TREASURES IN HEAVEN

TREASURES IN HEAVEN

KATHLEEN ALCALÁ

LATINO
VOICES

Northwestern University Press

Evanston, Illinois

Northwestern University Press
Evanston, Illinois 60208-4210

Northwestern University Press edition published 2003. Copyright © 2000 by Kathleen Alcalá. First published in hardcover by Chronicle Books, San Francisco, California, U.S.A. All rights reserved.

Printed in the United States of America

10 9 8 7 6 5 4 3 2 1

ISBN 0-8101-2036-4

The epigraph is excerpted from "Brindis: For the Barrio," from *Arise Chicano! and Other Poems* by Angela de Hoyos, 1975. Translation by Mireya Robles. Used by permission of the author and translator.

Designed by Pamela Geismar
Typeset by Candace Creasy, Blue Friday

Library of Congress Cataloging-in-Publication data are available from the Library of Congress.

For all our relations—
   by blood, by empathy, and by revolutionary spirit

ACKNOWLEDGMENTS

Many people helped bring this book to fruition. I would especially like to acknowledge the following for their assistance while I was researching and writing this novel: Lauro Flores, University of Washington; Ilan Stavans, Amherst College; and Ken Newman. In Mexico, Laura Barcia Lafuente of the Sindicato Nacional de Trabajadores de la Educación, Jorge González de Leon, Margo González, and Claire Joysmith all spent valuable time with me. Licenciada Guadalupe Ybarra Olvera of the Biblioteca Miguel Lerdo de Tejada, Fernando Lizarragas of the Hemeroteca at the Universidád de Mexico, and Doctora Luz Elena Gutiérrez de Velasco at the Programa Interdisciplinario de Estudios de la Mujer at the Colegio de México also rendered valuable assistance. I would like to thank the staff at the Centro de Documentacion Historica en el Centro Comunitario Nidjei Israel for allowing me access to archival material, and sharing family stories.

The works of Enrique Krauze, William H. Beezley, and Michael Johns were very helpful in understanding the complexity of culture during the Porfírian era. I would especially like to thank Anna Macías, the author of *Against All Odds: The Feminist Movement in Mexico to 1940*, Greenwood Press, 1982, for her personal kindness and for writing her book. It was the inspiration for *Treasures in Heaven*.

Por vez primera
la mesa puesta
con platos llenos de esperanza,
y en nuestros manos analfabetas
algún noble destino ha depositado
una dorada promesa para el mañana.

For once,
the table is set
with plates full of hope,
and in our illiterate hands
some kind fate has placed
a promise of gold for tomorrow.

—*Angela de Hoyos*

MONTE DE PIEDAD

Even the doves were in mourning. The trees seemed to sigh at her leave-taking, and the windows of each building looked, to her, like sorrowful eyes.

As Estela boarded the coach that would take her to Mexico City, and as it rolled slowly from the center of Saltillo and through the outlying villages, the houses becoming farther and farther apart until they dwindled to clusters around a water tank, then to the occasional hacienda—Buena Vista, Angostura, Encantanda—she wondered when she would see the city of her birth again. Even many years later, when she recounted her travels and adventures to me, she experienced a pang in her heart at recalling the last familiar landmark as it disappeared behind her in the dust.

Her sister would think she had lost her mind. That is one reason she had not said good-bye. Her father, Don Horacio, still unwell after his ordeal at the hands of the authorities, must have suspected her intent, and perhaps even condoned it, for he transferred additional funds to her account in the days before she left. Perhaps, she thought a little bitterly, he felt that his business would not suffer so much if all of the parties to the scandal—Zacarías, his parents, and his wife, Estela—were not to be seen for a while.

The road climbed through barrancas, steep, water-cut canyons, then ran level across great expanses of pastures and fields. The haciendas—La Ventura, San Salvador, el hacienda del Salado—unfolded before them like so many handkerchiefs laid end to end. When the horses needed water, the driver stopped at the estanques, offering the passengers much-needed relief as well.

At dusk, they stopped at the haciendas and were put up in rooms kept for that purpose. Estela and her elderly maid, Josefina, pushed furniture up against the door before going to bed, joking about the rancher who eyed them whenever his wife fell asleep.

They had nine fellow travelers, an empty seat affording a place for Noé to nap, or an extra spot for someone to stretch and doze for a bit. Endless rounds of cards occupied the days of the men, endless numbers of cigars, and from one señora and señor, endless amounts of bickering. Estela and Josefina alternated sitting by a window, which offered relief from the motion sickness induced by the constant bumping. Estela longed to sit on top with the driver, as the men sometimes did, but did not want to draw undue attention to herself. At least three in the carriage knew who she was, but pretended that they did not. Estela did not pay much heed. In her mind, she replayed over and over her parting with Zacarías, her apprehension of Victoria coming into the house with her shoes and stockings in hand, the wedding at which she and Dr. Victor Carranza saw to the marriage of Victoria and the young soldier.

Never to be for us, she thought, love of my life, yet never to be for us.

Estela had not known what to pack for the journey, since she had no idea what she would do once she arrived. She had a vague notion that people would meet her and, seeing that she meant well—or at least no harm—conduct her to a safe place to stay until she could make some decisions.

She had packed four dresses, two hats, and two pairs of boots. She had brought a good coat, a nightgown, and a set of four plates she had inherited from her grandmother and which she had always loved. She brought an extra shawl, clothes for Noé, and a parasol. She brought a valuable piece of her mother's jewelry, hidden in a false compartment in the trunk. Estela also brought one book of poetry that she read and reread on the coach, a book about a beloved who could never be obtained, about death transforming us into a part of nature, and other rich, dark, brooding thoughts. Its author, Manuel Acuña, son of Saltillo, had shot himself over a married woman in Mexico City some years earlier, ending a potential medical career. In death he was famous and, as he predicted, a part of the Mexican landscape.

When she could, Estela slept, and when she woke, her heart ached—for what, she could not say. Of course, her heart ached for all of the happy conjunctions we all wish for, to live out our lives in the place of our choice with the person of our choice, perhaps to raise happy, healthy children, to hear the birds sing, and be greeted with respect by one's neighbors. But as with most of us, this was not to be. And so Estela traveled on across the sprawling, mysterious country of Mexico, here and there densely peopled, but otherwise slumbering in its neglect, like the innocent daughter of a rural farmer, unaware of her dark and careless beauty.

In a way, over these endless miles, Estela's mind fell back into the dreaming slumber it had occupied before she met Victor Carranza, when she thought that she was relatively happy in her marriage. It was a sort of dreamworld filled with exotic images and half-implied romances. San Luis Potosí, with its eighteen towers and domes, sparked an extended day-dream of Moorish principalities. San Miguel de Allende put her in mind of a medieval village, and its constantly tolling bells kept her from sleeping during the night spent there.

She allowed Josefina and the other passengers to entertain Noé with their carryings-on, and she only took him to nurse him to sleep under her shawl now and then. But he was growing quickly and would not need her in this capacity much longer. Estela dared not think about what she had left behind, lest she change her mind and return. She did not want to go over the circumstances that had led a woman of good background and upbringing to leave her home, her family, and everything she had ever known. And she could not begin to apprehend what lay before her.

They entered the tragic and beautiful city of Querétaro, where the reign of the Emperor Maxmiliano had ended. He gave gold pieces to the execution squad, it was said, with his own image on them, so that they would shoot straight and not leave him to suffer. A little farther on was the garden with the famous statue of Herculus—said to have cost fifteen thousand dollars in Italy—surrounding a huge cotton mill known by the same name as the statue.

At a wooded rise of over nine thousand feet, past the hacienda of Arroyo Zarco, the plateau began to fall again towards the approach to the Valley of Mexico. As they crossed the causeway of San Cosmé, and before entering the city gate, they were stopped by uniformed men who, after much discussion with the driver, charged a fee to enter the city. Each passenger gave up a few pesos, and only after they were safely past the roadblock did Estela understand from the conversation that they had been robbed. Apparently this was such a common occurrence that everyone else had been expecting it.

"Welcome to Mexico City," said the rancher's wife. "If you are planning to spend any time here, you better get used to it."

"Every officer takes his bite," agreed her husband.

"But who did they work for?" asked Estela. "Were they police? Or were they army officers?"

"Who knows?" responded the rancher. "They were probably left over from the French intervention. And who knows

which side they fought on at that time." This brought a round
of chuckles.

"Everyone is always on the side in power," responded someone else. "Just remember that."

As they continued on their way, the driver called out that
they were passing the house built by Hernán Cortés himself on
the left, but Estela was unable to see it from her seat.

✴

It was a time of great progress in Mexico City. It was a time of
railroads and matching silver tea services; first-class horses,
imported wines, and French Revivalist architecture. It was a
time to discuss politics, international economics, and the graces
of the perfect woman. Every rail line led to Mexico City—
every stage coach line, every cattle drive, and every goat track.

It was also a time of starvation, of forced marches and sum-
mary executions. Those without money had no voice and
would soon have no land. To be a woman without family was
to be derided, degraded, and disgraced. Born into misery, a
woman brought her children into it, ate it with her tortillas,
and was buried in it. Even those of good family were judged,
by the law of the land, to be *imbecilis sexus,* imbeciles by virtue
of their sex, requiring guardians for themselves and their
properties—if not fathers or husbands, then lawyers or even
their own sons.

The city was vast with possibilities, voracious for new blood
to spill on top of old, relentless in its consumption of power and
labor. People jostled for a place near the top, and those in the
know stayed at the Hotel Iturbide. It was the only lodging of
which Estela had ever heard, and so upon arriving, she hired
a carriage and asked to be taken there.

The room was large and sumptuous, the service perfect.
People came and went in the lobby escorted by their servants,
dressed for morning, afternoon, or evening. They discussed

their latest visits to Europe or New York or Chicago, and the more fashionable had undergone psychiatric analysis in Vienna. Estela was in awe of even the hired help at the Hotel Iturbide, dressed in matching livery, and whose language and manners far outshone her own. There was the faintest air of contempt about them for her, nothing that could be remarked on, only the pulled-down corner of a mouth upon hearing her pronunciation of the mother language. As for the society people, because they did not know her, Estela was invisible.

At the end of the first week, Estela asked to see her bill. It took all of her money to pay it, money she had thought would last several months. Estela directed Josefina to pack and asked to be taken to "a moderate boardinghouse." The driver appraised the party, then took them to a different part of the District, farther north from the Alameda. The streets grew narrower and more crowded with people on foot, the voices louder, riderless donkeys and ownerless dogs more numerous.

When the carriage pulled up in front of a large, featureless building, Josefina turned away to reach into a private part of her garments. She paid the driver in silver, who said, "Ask for la casera, Señora Gomez."

La casera turned out to be an older woman with a pinched face who wanted to see a little more plata before she would show them a room. She wore a faded dress and a large ring of keys around her wrist. Their trunk was carried in by a boy and deposited in a bare room with a single iron bed. La casera recited the house rules—no overnight guests, no drinking or loud behavior, and the outer door was locked at nine each evening, upon the ringing of the bells of San Lorenzo Martir. She eyed them suspiciously, as if to drive home her points, before leaving them to unpack. Estela wanted Josefina to stay there with the baby, but Josefina insisted on accompanying her mistress on the next, pressing errand. And so the three of them went, on foot, to El Monte de Piedad.

It was a vast building in the very center of Mexico, built practically on the bleeding heart of the old temple. Across from it stood the Cathedral, bearing witness to the ascendancy of the Church in this exotic and barbarous place.

El Monte itself, built in the 1700s, had been erected by a kind soul, the Count of Regla, who saw the need of the poor to be able to obtain cash. By leaving a clock or a bracelet, a firearm or a finely wrought piece of art, the poor of Mexico—those without papers or bank accounts or properties, those without deeds or contracts or even last names—could trust their goods to a clerk in exchange for plata. With luck, they could redeem their valuables before they were sold to junk speculators and reappeared on the Street of Thieves, for all to see and handle, and perhaps for someone else to buy.

It was to this edifice, this monument to the vagaries of fortune in this life, that Estela, Josefina, and Noé repaired. Estela unrolled the length of black velvet she had concealed on her person and revealed her mother's treasure to the young clerk in gold-filled spectacles. The sudden play of light upon the faceted gems of the necklace was startling, and the clerk made as if to shield the display not from his own eyes, but from those of passersby, by encompassing it in the crook of his arm.

With a practiced motion, he flipped up his spectacles and clamped his eye around a jeweler's glass, appraising the piece for a long moment, then turning it over to read the mark of the maker on its clasp, checking for any flaws in the gems or setting.

He looked again at the two women, in sober but respectable clothing, and the little boy, and decided against calling the authorities. They had probably come by this piece honestly, he deduced, based on his already extensive experience with such things.

"But señora," he asked finally, "why do you come here with this? Surely you can obtain a loan from a bank, can pay a lower interest than we will by necessity be forced to charge."

Estela looked at him. "I know no one in this city," she said. "I have not eaten today. Will a banker give me money for a room for tonight?"

The clerk nodded thoughtfully. "Just a minute," he said, and disappeared into one of the many doorways that divided the giant building into an infinity of small spaces. He returned with another man, who again appraised the necklace, and Estela.

"We will write you a contract," said the older man. "We do not want to be responsible for separating you from such an important piece, no doubt a family heirloom?" He paused and Estela nodded. "So we will give you a long-term contract at a slightly lower rate."

"Bueno," said Estela.

The young clerk, under the older man's instructions, began the tedious process of writing out a loan agreement. Then he read it aloud to Estela, who momentarily wished for the advice and presence of her old legal counsel, Licenciado Ernesto Vargas. Upon hearing the interest rate to be charged over the course of a year, she looked at Josefina, who nodded gravely, suddenly an expert in such matters. Estela signed the papers, and the younger clerk began to count out the money to her, the older man counting silently along with him. It seemed to be an enormous amount, with stacks and stacks of bills growing on the counter.

The moment he had finished, the clerk whisked the money into a plain leather envelope, suitable for carrying legal papers, as though anxious to remove the cash from view.

"Now," said the older clerk. "One word of advice. Go directly to a bank and open an account. The cash of even provincials is welcome at any bank."

Estela thought she almost detected a smile. "Thank you," she said. "I will do that."

"A su servicio," said the clerk, bowing slightly. "Buena suerta."

Estela could use luck from any quarter, and she gladly accepted his blessing. The portfolio between them, Josefina carrying Noé on one hip, Estela and Josefina made their way out of El Monte de Piedad and onto the jam-packed streets.

"All of the people in the world seem to be on this street," said Estela nervously. They made their way down the walkway, carried along by the crowd, until they came to what seemed to be a bank, entered it, and discovered that it was, in fact, a bank.

Estela asked to open an account, something she had never done, and another clerk was summoned to take down the information. Her name elicited no special response, but her recently acquired address produced a pause. Estela realized that she should have done this while staying at the fine hotel.

When asked her marital status, Estela opened her mouth and answered, "Widow."

"Deceased husband's name," asked the clerk.

"Zacarías Carabajál de la Cueva y Vargas."

"Date and place of his death."

"April 1877. Casas Grandes, Chihuahua. He was killed in an Indian uprising." Whether it was true or not, that was the month her life had changed forever.

"And he named you custodian of his estate?"

"Yes." She did not mention that she had gained control of it earlier, with the help of their solicitor. The less said about these things, the better, she felt.

Estela had thought about all of this during the long coach ride south. She decided it was easiest to say that she was a widow. And after all, she might as well be widowed, as much use as a husband was who had been driven into exile by the authorities.

As the clerk at El Monte de Piedad had predicted, the bank was all too happy to take custody of her money.

The trio went out again, Noé now fussing and fitful, and secured a carriage. They bought a few things along the way, and upon returning to their room, fell upon the bread and cheese like ravenous animals. Although the room was bare of all but a bed and bureau—Josefina curled up on a mat on the floor—Estela felt more at ease than she had at the hotel. The people there reminded her of who she was not. Also, she did not know why, but her mother's necklace had seemed to weigh upon her, like a burden from the past. In doing one more unforgivable thing, she felt that she had divested herself of a last anchor to the respectable life she had left behind. Estela slept well that night for the first time since arriving in Mexico City.

LA SEÑORITA

As Estela and Josefina soon discovered, the boarders near San Lorenzo were forbidden to consume pulque or make excessive noise unless they bribed the casera first. Each Friday evening, the music teacher upstairs—the one with the young and nubile wife—held a dance by subscription. All manner of behavior was tolerated as long as the casera was given a sweet or a biscuit or a bit of cheese in exchange for unlocking the door for the stream of lively visitors. The dances ended more or less at two in the morning, at which point the dramas begun on the premises moved out to the street, usually in search of more pulque.

The rest of the week, Estela and Josefina learned entirely too much about their neighbors based solely on what could be heard through the thin walls. After a month of the squalor and din of the boardinghouse, Josefina begged Estela to overcome her scruples and contact Dr. Carranza.

"But how?" asked Estela. "I don't know where he is."

"The same way you would in Saltillo," she answered. "Write him a letter and give it to a boy."

But Estela could not bring herself to write to him. She tried and failed several times. Finally she went to a professional scribe, those men who sit with their little desks and pen and ink in every plaza, at the service of the abandoned, the lovesick, and those far from home.

Estela felt like all three. When she sat down in the chair opposite the scribe, her hands clasped in her lap, her story came pouring out, all in a jumble of names and places, dates and colors, feelings, emotions, and suppositions.

After careful consideration, this is what the scribe wrote:

My dear Dr. Carranza:
It is with great trepidation that I address you, not knowing your circumstances in Mexico City.

After the horrendous events in Saltillo, in which my own father was accused of aiding a fugitive from the law and refusing to cooperate with the authorities, my husband (the fugitive in question) fled for his life and is probably gone forever. He led me to believe that I will never hear from him again.

And after much agitation and much heartache, I have concluded that this is for the best. We were never meant to live out our lives together, and he has gone to seek whatever it is in God's name that he seeks.

And so, given the turmoil of my life, the shame and scandal attached to my home and family, and the fact that most of my children are grown and able to care for themselves, I have taken the almost unbelievable step of coming to Mexico.

I beg of you to forgive me for the impertinence of writing to you, but I know no one here—I am alone in the world with my baby, the only man in the world who has been faithful to me.

If I dare to say it, my feelings for you have remained unchanged. You have been like a lamp in the darkness to me, a beacon in the dark storm of my sorrows.

Again, please forgive me for this intrusion. If you wish to reach me, the bearer of this letter can direct you to me.

>   *With respect,*
>   *Mme. Carabajál Quintanilla*

"Is there an address for a reply?" he asked, pen poised above the letter.

"No, señor," she answered. "I would like any reply to be through you."

"Bueno," he answered, and summoned one of the urchins who loitered about in order to deliver missives to every part of the city and, at times, beyond.

Estela brought a little food back for Josefina and Noé, but the boy was restless and unwell.

"Living like this does not suit him," said Josefina, trying to lull the child to sleep. "He needs fresh air and water."

Estela placed a hand on her son's brow, then stood listening to the roiling life all around them—vendors outside hawked butter, violins, charcoal. Earlier she had seen a child in the street lifting human feces to his lips before his mother slapped it away. She resolved never to let go of Noé's hand while they were outside. Estela was ready to return home to Saltillo, to pretend that she had visited the city merely to take in the sights, to broaden herself.

While Noé was unhappy, he did not appear to have a fever. "I will massage his belly for him," she said, taking the boy from Josefina and placing him on the bed. "Sana sana, colita de rana," Estela intoned in a singsong voice as she rubbed circles on the boy's stomach. "Si no sanas ahora, sanarás mañana."

Estela did not sleep well that night, so many things running through her head, listening to her son as he slept fitfully.

The next day at precisely the time she had visited before, Estela returned to the scribe. He smiled broadly and handed her an envelope. It wasn't always so. More often than not, people came back day after day, entire lifetimes passed waiting for the answer sí or no.

After paying the scribe, Estela stepped a discreet distance
away before opening the heavy buff envelope with trembling
hands.

My dear,
Please do me the honor of meeting me tomorrow at La copa de
leche south of the Zócalo.
                        Dr. Victor Carranza

Estela arrived exactly forty-five minutes after the appointed
time. She did not wish to appear too eager, yet could not risk
that he would give up on her. Upon seeing him, after the lapse
of two years, Estela could barely look upon his countenance.
He was more handsome than ever, although he appeared a bit
worn. She refused to think of herself as subject to time and
cares as well.

They drank coffee and spoke quietly, yet said little. Each
was afraid to learn too much about the other. They agreed to
meet again.

On their second meeting, they took a carriage a few blocks
to a pensión. They loved with urgency, the sense of time stolen
from the present, time owed to them from the past. Now it
seemed natural; it would have been unnatural, perverse, even,
if they had not done so. After all this time, they allowed themselves a freedom they had not felt before.

Victor began by removing Estela's clothes. As she lay supine
beside him, he took a pale rose tinged with red from a vase
beside the bed and ran its face lightly over Estela's body.
Gently, gently, not allowing the sharp thorns to touch her skin,
he caressed her over and over with the whispering petals, from
the crown of her head to the soles of her feet. He grazed the surface of her skin and raised her florid nipples. He explored the

secret folds and warm curves of her body with this third hand, this seeking eye, as she lay in a near swoon.

Tirelessly, relentlessly, he raised every nerve in her body with the gossamer touch of the flower until she felt that she must rise and levitate toward the ceiling, weightless with desire. Then, gazing upon her, Victor removed and solemnly ate each of the petals as though taking Communion, pressing a few between Estela's lips and teeth as well. Only then did he remove his own clothing and lie down with her to begin to try to satisfy their passion.

After some time, Victor Carranza caressed Estela's breasts— riper, now, since the birth of her last child—and dreamed over her body. Afternoon light filtered through the shuttered windows, along with the quiet sounds of siesta.

"You know that I am married," he said quietly.

Estela's heart stopped momentarily. She had been near dozing in the warmth and satisfaction that followed their lovemaking.

"No, I did not," she said. She had not wanted to know. Until now, she had refused to think about it.

Carranza stroked her gently, absently. "And we have a child."

The use of the word *we* chilled her.

Estela reached for and pulled her shawl over her body. "I did not ask you for anything," she said.

"I know," he answered, shifting his hand to her hair, where it had freed itself around her face. "But I thought you should know. I don't want there to be secrets between us."

Estela began to cry in short, quiet sobs. She sat up and curled her arms around her knees.

"I wish I knew someone here," she said. "There is nothing left for me in Saltillo."

"But you *do* know someone," he said. "Me."

"I mean *really* know someone. Someone who can acknowledge me, show me things, help me find a place to live and how to support myself."

"I can do those things," he whispered.

"No!" she said. "I did not move here to live in la casa chica, the little house where you keep your mistress." More quietly she said, "I have a little money. From my father. My own. But I gave my house to my daughters."

"And your oldest son?"

"He is gone. He has joined a religious sect and left us and all of his worldly goods behind. My sister wrote to me and told me."

After a bit Carranza said, "I would never do you any disrespect." His voice was gentle and even. "I will introduce you to people who can be helpful. It will compromise neither of us. I would be honored to do so," he added, "if you will let me."

✶

And so Estela came to meet La Señorita Mejora de Gonga. Carranza introduced Estela to "La Señorita," which is what most people called her. La Señorita never asked Estela about her deceased husband, understanding that many women were widowed under mysterious and complicated circumstances in Mexico in those days.

La Señorita, on the other hand, had been born into wealth and refused to relinquish it to suitors or lawyers, land speculators or empresarios, priests or adventurers. She invested it wisely and gave generously to those causes that attracted her attention. And she dressed well, eschewing the rage for Parisian fashion in favor of a classic line designed especially for her diminutive figure by her dressmaker. It seemed to consist of black costumes with elaborate pleats and hidden pockets that allowed her to pull fans or lorgnettes out, then have them vanish again without a trace. This added to her aura of self-sufficiency.

La Señorita immediately approved of Estela because of her modest and practical approach to dress, prior to now always judged as rather plain and unimaginative by her sister and daughters. But La Señorita took her to be a useful person, since La Señorita divided all people into two categories—useful and useless.

While Carranza could easily have been dismissed on the basis of his exceedingly good looks as useless, La Señorita was more astute than that. Because Carranza was a doctor with a generous and liberal approach to his calling, La Señorita had classified him as useful to her most important cause— the plight of women in Mexico. She did not always know how she would put him to use. At times she referred women in need of special care to him; at other times, she relied on his society connections. As with others of her acquaintance, La Señorita kept the doctor in reserve, like a jack in a good round of poker.

Carranza left the two women in the tea-room of the Hotel Iturbide. Where before Estela had been invisible, now, in the company of La Señorita, she drew many admiring and curious glances.

La Señorita was all business. "My understanding is that you are from the provinces, a woman of quality, who has come on her own to Mexico."

"Yes," said Estela hesitantly, "I hope I am of quality."

La Señorita ignored this response. "Can you read and write?" she asked.

"Yes, I can," said Estela more firmly.

"Very well, then. I am starting a school for poor children, children who are all but orphans because of the circumstances of their parentage. You understand?"

"Yes," said Estela, though at that time, she thought La Señorita meant merely that they were very poor.

"Right now they come to my home, where a young woman from a good family who can barely read or write tutors them. But we need someone more mature, with maternal experience, who can not only instruct them in letters, but can see that they get enough to eat and can teach them manners as well—the process of civilization that can transform them from the inside out according to the precepts of Erasmo of Rotterdam. They need practical skills to see them through the world. Especially the girls. And we need to find a larger, more permanent place for the school."

Estela wondered at all of this. She was vaguely aware of a booklet on etiquette consulted by older ladies in Saltillo by an Erasmo. "Practical skills?" She was not sure if she herself had any.

"Yes, yes," said La Señorita impatiently. "Sewing. Weaving. Doing sums."

"Well, I can sew a little."

"Oh, you don't need to have mastered these things. I need someone to hire instructors, to oversee the whole thing. Like running a large household. You have run a household, haven't you?" La Señorita produced a tortoise-shell lorgnette and looked at Estela as though the evidence of it would show.

"Oh, of course! That I can do," she answered, as if suddenly seeing the light.

"Very well, then. We shall begin tomorrow." La Señorita turned away from Estela as though dismissing her and motioned to her driver.

"Where are you staying?" she asked. "We can take you back."

When Estela told her, La Señorita frowned. Estela explained that she was unfamiliar with the city and had done the best she could with her limited resources.

"That won't do at all," La Señorita declared. "We will pick up your child and your belongings and you will stay with me." She stood and added, "I have a very large house."

And so she did. La Señorita held a handkerchief over her nose against the reek of the street where Estela was staying, and Josefina was only too glad to hand Noé up to Estela and climb into the fine carriage herself. Their trunk was loaded on the back and deposited in a fine, sunny room south of the Alameda, on the Paseo de Bucareli, where La Señorita's house turned out to be, as she promised, a large, imposing structure of a variety of architectural influences. Its rococo and baroque exterior, its Victorian dormers and French Gothic casements, supported by Corinthian columns and screened by Moroccan friezes, stood in contrast to La Señorita's simple and elegant figure. The house made her seem like a visitor from the future, and much as she was at home, La Señorita always seemed about to take flight for an age that could accommodate her modern ideas.

Estela learned, gradually, that La Señorita Mejora de Gonga was the sun of her own solar system, and the lesser planets approached and spun away as they suited her or complied with her bidding. She seemed to be at the center of a vast network of businesses, romances, and political intrigues.

People confessed things to La Señorita that they would not dare tell others, not even their priests, secure in the knowledge that she would not divulge their secrets. Yet a nod here, a well-placed bribe there, and they could see their own wills and aspirations—if in keeping with La Señorita's—gradually turn the tide of events. Or perhaps they only imagined that this was so.

This influence was exercised in interior places, sparkling drawing rooms, dimly lit boudoirs, in the form of well-timed words or the slightest movement of a hand. In other words, her power was subterranean, implied, and so of the greatest potency.

And yet La Señorita wore this lightly—caught up in the moment that was about to occur, she was constantly in motion. She appeared to be of a constant age, though no one could remember when she had not had great influence. She had an impeccable pedigree that stretched back to when "the kings of Spain lived in caves," as one wag put it, but she never trotted out her inherited titles, as some people did even in a free Mexico. In fact, La Señorita managed to deflect almost all questions about her private life, always turning the conversation back onto her interlocutor in a way that was both flattering and devious.

Being in her presence acted as a sort of narcotic, from which people later awoke and realized that they had pledged money to support a school or hospital, or to donate clothing to the poor. La Señorita wheeled through it all, a blackbird on the wind, and had Estela known more about her, she might have been daunted by the prospect of becoming her assistant. But La Señorita saw in Estela the perfect combination of naïveté and intelligence, individual will and compliance, to suit her purposes.

LA ESCUELA DE PACIENCIA

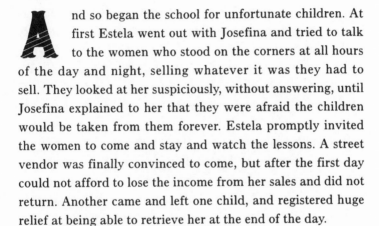nd so began the school for unfortunate children. At first Estela went out with Josefina and tried to talk to the women who stood on the corners at all hours of the day and night, selling whatever it was they had to sell. They looked at her suspiciously, without answering, until Josefina explained to her that they were afraid the children would be taken from them forever. Estela promptly invited the women to come and stay and watch the lessons. A street vendor was finally convinced to come, but after the first day could not afford to lose the income from her sales and did not return. Another came and left one child, and registered huge relief at being able to retrieve her at the end of the day.

Estela found La Señorita to be almost supernatural in her efficiency, seeming not to even sleep. Often, late at night, Estela heard her carriage going out, not to return until the early hours of the morning. Yet La Señorita was always up and dressed the next day, never remarking upon her nocturnal adventures, nor stinting from the many tasks she set for herself each day.

Waiting each morning in her parlor—which held, next to the high windows, a feminine writing desk and a credenza overflowing with papers—was her secretary, accountant, and solicitor, Licenciado Humberto Lizarraga de Avila. A large man of infinite patience, Don Humberto always had a list that had been prepared with La Señorita at the end of the previous day. As each appointment or activity was finished, La Señorita would wave in his direction, and he would read off the next. A letter to answer, a good word to be put in for a family fallen on hard times, an audience with an assistant to Don Porfírio—the lists never ended, only continued to the next day. Even with the shouting and laughter of the children outside, La Señorita continued her work uninterrupted, leaving only to attend to urgent business elsewhere.

Word spread that the giant house on the Paseo de Bucareli harbored buena gente. Some brought their ragged children and lingered outside of the house until the police chased them off or the lessons ended, but once they knew they could get their children back, more came and left children in Estela's charge. The school was held in the patio of La Señorita's expansive home, and Estela loved to sit by the fountain and teach lessons to the children.

It soon became evident that the children needed more than lessons in grammar and sums, however, and Estela arranged to have a woman bathe and distribute fresh clothing to the children once a week. La Señorita's gardener was not happy at this use of his territory, and they all contracted fleas on a regular basis. Still, liberal amounts of soap did wonders for the well-being of both the children and the adults who worked with them. Estela soon turned over the daily lessons to her assistant, Corona, a poor but well-born young woman who possessed the rudiments of an education. Her father had been a schoolteacher before he died, leaving a widow and five children.

Once a month, around nine o'clock in the morning, a different group of children showed up for classes. They were not always the same children, but there was a core of them who were the same. They came all at once, as though there were a special coach that collected them from the slums of Mexico and deposited them at La Señorita's doorstep. They did not appear any better or worse off than the children who were already at the school—some appearing fed, others not fed, dressed or underdressed. Some were there for the day; some stayed for a month or so, then left again. Others came and stayed.

"Where do they come from?" Estela had asked.

"They are the children of the desafortunados," was the answer La Señorita gave her, but this was the same answer she gave to almost all of Estela's questions. Everyone was the child of an unfortunate. If La Señorita did not use this phrase in a descriptive manner as applied to her charges, then she tended to apply it to her enemies as a curse.

Estela wondered at this, but did not know the answer to the mystery until the day that she happened to step outside at the moment when they arrived.

Sometime during the previous year, the government had decreed that the women of pleasure of Mexico City should be registered. What's more, it was ordered that, for the safety of the public, these women should be examined by a physician once a month to see that they were fit and healthy and free of communicable diseases. Those who were not were to be kept at the public hospital until they were well again.

This led to what was called "the parade," which took place every week on a rotating basis, prior to the weekend, when, it was assumed, the women would be most actively employed. It happened that the parade lined up within a few blocks of La Señorita's establishment, which was not too far from the Department of Public Health.

Estela happened out that particular morning in time to see several flamboyantly dressed women kissing their children good-bye in front of the school. Twirling their parasols, they left in a group, arm in arm, to the catcalls of men loitering in the street. Instead of the stony stares or pointed ignorance that was expected of a well-brought-up woman, this group threw kisses and suggestions for convenient times to meet them later. They walked with confidence, sin vergüenza.

"But why didn't you tell me who these children belong to?" Estela asked La Señorita.

"Why does it matter?" she countered. "Would you educate them differently?"

"But they are hardly unfortunate. Those women make more money than some of the men in Mexico."

"Does it make you uncomfortable?" asked La Señorita. "Those children would not be in school were it not for us. Would you have them accompany their mothers on the street?"

"But most of them don't come to school except on . . . those days. Where are they the rest of the time?"

"In a room," said La Señorita. "Or on the street. Or waiting to be fed. Why do you think that district is called El Niño Perdido?"

The light began to dawn for Estela. "And the other children in the school? They are not really orphans, are they?"

"Some are, and some wish that they were." La Señorita stood up from her desk and began to pace. "Those women lining up for the exam are only the registered prostitutes. There are thousands more either less fortunate or more discreet."

Estela looked down in embarrassment. "I had no idea there were so many women of bad reputation in the city." No wonder, she thought, that people in Saltillo thought it scandalous to even visit, much less live here.

"This status has nothing to do with a woman's virtue, kindness, goodness, or nobility," said La Señorita. "In fact, it has nothing to do with women at all. It is strictly a matter between men, like most things in Mexico. A man wants nothing to do with that which another man has tasted or used. It is a matter of property, of territory."

Humberto shifted in his seat but did not interrupt.

"The streets of Mexico teem with women who have been tasted, then abandoned, by men. Often they are brought into a household at twelve or thirteen to watch the children or do laundry. A pretty one is soon forced behind the cooking shed by the patrón or oldest son. She is warned not to tell, or she will lose her position. But sooner or later her belly begins to swell, and she finds herself on the street with no more regard than an abandoned dog. These young women do what they have to in order to survive."

"Mexico is now home to over ten thousand prostitutes, more than in Paris," added Humberto quietly.

"We are the laughingstock of Europe," said La Señorita, "of those people whom we pain ourselves to emulate."

"But can't they go back to their villages?" asked Estela.

"Their fate would be the same there, with the addition of shaming their families."

Estela realized that this was true. Even now, just by coming to Mexico City by herself, it would be awkward for her to return to Saltillo.

"Instead, with no other skills, and a child to support, they join the other leperos on the streets. If they earn money, they can rent a room for the night, or buy some food. If not, then they sleep on the streets."

"The legislators, rather than calling for reforms, try to restrict their rights," said Humberto sternly.

"Those men," said La Señorita, looking out the window to where Corona led the children in a recitation, "who sit in Congress, attend Mass, and march in uniform for the glory of la pátria, are the fathers of these children." She jabbed at the window with her fan for emphasis. "Those are the men who pull the noose braided of laws and religious proscriptions tighter and tighter around the necks of the women of Mexico.

Meanwhile, they continue to support their legitimate children and share their titles and venereal diseases with their lawful wives."

"So that's why the medical exams," said Estela in a wondering voice. "To protect the men."

"Exactly!" said La Señorita. "It certainly would not be to protect the women!" La Señorita continued to look out the window, gripping her fan tightly. After a moment, she seemed to regain control of her emotions. "So you see," she said, turning and smiling at Estela, "the work we do is very important. If we do not help, no one else will."

Estela smiled wanly and excused herself. Humberto, who had returned to his smiling self, stood and smiled warmly as she left. She could not help but wonder why this particular cause, of all the desperate situations around them, was the closest to La Señorita's heart.

✱

Estela returned to her classroom with her newfound knowledge. She tried not to, but found herself wondering about some of the older girls who had come into her charge.

"Why are you staring at me that way?" asked Rebeca one day. She was a girl of about thirteen with beautiful, creamy skin. There was just a tinge of insolence in her voice.

Estela recovered herself. "Try to round your *s*'s more," she said, as though deeply interested in her penmanship. "They look like little boxes."

The next month, Rebeca's mother came for her, and she was not seen again.

"What will happen to her?" asked Estela, afraid of the answer.

"What do you think?" answered La Señorita.

"But can't we stop her? Can't we tell the authorities?" Even as she asked, Estela could hear the futility of her words.

"Stop her from what? The girl is her own child. We could insist that the women give up all rights to their children, and I have considered it. But then they would be afraid to bring them here in the first place. Those who have not been back to get their children drink or die or don't care."

More softly, La Señorita said, "Most don't have daughters as beautiful as Rebeca. May God go with her."

For the first time in her life, that night, Estela wept for someone other than herself.

✷

The next day, she presented herself in La Señorita's parlor, where she did most of her business. It was a glorious day, and the canaries in cages were singing. Humberto sat in an easy chair smoking his pipe.

"I think I have a solution to the problem," said Estela.

"A solution? To the problems of Mexico? Sit down." La Señorita waved her towards a chair. Estela could never tell if La Señorita was mocking her or not.

Estela took a deep breath. "We must educate the mothers as well."

"The mothers? Of our children? Go on."

"We must offer school for grown women, or at least girls who have left their parents' homes. They come to the city to work, alone, without knowledge or protection, without money. They think they will go to work in the homes of the rich. And they do. But they have no idea what will happen to them. Many of them are barely older than children themselves."

As she spoke, Estela began to see her own plan. "They can come here and stay with us. We could even place them in respectable homes, families with references."

"References?" said La Señorita. "Who do you think give references? Saints?"

"No, no," said Humberto, holding up his hand. "Let her speak."

Estela rushed on. "And even as they work, perhaps they could take classes with us, in cooking or sewing, or . . . or type-setting. Or teaching."

"Typesetting?" said La Señorita. She turned her back and began to look out the window, as though she had lost interest in the conversation.

"We need to catch them before they become used to the street. Before they become borrachas to forget what is done to them."

That provoked a brief silence. Humberto puffed thoughtfully.

"Who would teach them?" he asked.

"I can teach them reading and writing," said Estela. "Corona is seventeen. She knows enough now to teach the younger children. We could hire people to teach specific trades, useful trades. The papers are full every day of advertisements for skilled workers."

"Skilled *men*," said Humberto.

"We could start our own factory," said La Señorita to the birds in their cages. "Perhaps the women could learn to sew and make clothing for children." She turned to face them, and Estela saw, for the first time, the enthusiasm in her face. "It could help support the school."

Estela smiled, and the birds sang the praises of her idea.

La Señorita had already directed Estela to look for a larger building for the children's school. It had long ago outgrown her own courtyard, where the children trampled her flowers and frightened the songbirds. Estela, accompanied by Josefina, had inquired of a real-estate broker of the availability of such a building, and been escorted to first one, then another edifice of wildly varying descriptions—from mansions to old ranchos, an abandoned pulquería to an empty knitting factory.

Estela was amazed at the array of old and dilapidated buildings that abounded in the Capital. As many people as there
were, she had expected that every empty space would have
been filled up. But these were spaces that required rent, so
much of the population remained on the street, or rented rooms
by the night when they could afford it.

Finally she was shown a former cloister, and the peaceful
courtyard, with its glimpse of sky above the roofline of the top-
most floor, struck her as just right. Unlike La Señorita's house,
its lines were simple and straightforward. It had been designed
in a simpler era, one Estela was unable to place, when God's
presence was to be evoked by stillness, not motion. It was not
too far from the working-class part of town, yet had a sturdy
outer gate that would secure it from the night. As Estela
walked through it, pigeons flew up from the courtyard where
they had made themselves at home. A few families appeared to
be camped in its rooms, but they had not damaged the edifice
too badly in their pursuit of firewood and furniture.

"Esta lo es," she declared. This is it.

Humberto and La Señorita came to see for themselves and
agreed. Arrangements were made through the Archbishop's
offices to lease the former cloister.

Estela wanted to call it La Escuela de María Magdalena, but
La Señorita held out hope that respectable girls would come to
the school, too—girls who did not yet have to invoke "the other
María" in their prayers. So it was called La Escuela de la
Paciencia de la Madre de Dios. The classes for children, located
in the second-floor rooms, were called simply La Escuelita.

Those with children could drop them off before attending
classes themselves, and many a child spent the better part of
the day in the courtyard of the edifice, first in his or her own
classes, then late into the night when their mothers came from

work to study on their own behalf. Sometimes Estela came across a child sleeping peacefully on the stone balcony, flung out on the hard stone as though in a luxurious bed. She learned not to wake these children or try to make them more comfortable, because they inevitably jumped to their feet, fiercely awake, determined to defend themselves from the predators of the street they had come to fear.

A woman was engaged to stand all day in a corner of the courtyard cooking tortillas, a pot of beans always boiling, collecting centavos here or there from the grateful, tired mothers. She, too, brought her children, and the older two soon began to attend the classes in conversation and the practical sciences that were offered, free, to them. A skinny yellow cat was turned loose in the courtyard to make the pigeons feel less at home, and the former cloister, bereft for years of its chaste inhabitants, began to provide a new life for the "children of the unfortunate."

MATRACAS

A s more women came to La Paciencia, Corona would approach Estela, eyes averted, with questions about what to do in this case or that. Often, Estela had no more idea than she did. But Hermelinda, stirring her pot of beans in the corner, would laugh and say, "Don't be so serious, Corona. There is always a way. Let me go and talk to her." And she would leave Corona stirring the beans while she took the new woman aside for a few moments.

In the morning, having already lit her fire and begun making tortillas before dawn, Hermelinda would shout compliments and encouragement to the women as they left for their own food stands or domestic jobs.

"Míra que bonita," she would say. "I bet you didn't get that blouse by being demure!"

"Everything in this life is paid for!" would come the reply, and they would all laugh raucously.

Everyone felt better around Hermelinda. "You see these lines on my face?" she would say. "They are smile lines because God has let me see another day." Estela saw even the most dejected of women eventually smile and give way to Hermelinda's sunny disposition.

At first Estela was a little offended by her sensibilities, and wondered if people would get the wrong impression if they visited the school and heard Hermelinda carrying on. It might sound as though they were encouraging these women to continue in their loose ways. But Estela soon realized that no one was going to visit the school who didn't have urgent business there. There was no society into which to introduce the women of La Paciencia, and their needs were of the most basic sort, the three wishes of the poor woman who gave coins to the temple in Jesus' parable—appealing to Divine Providence that she not lack shelter, clothing, or sustenance.

Eventually, Estela realized that she needed someone like Hermelinda as her assistant, and spoke with La Señorita about hiring her. Hermelinda had the experience that Estela and Corona, in their relatively sheltered lives, lacked in dealing with women with more bitter histories. La Señorita agreed, and a new woman soon stood stirring the bean pot, while Hermelinda, with decisiveness and aplomb, helped Estela with the more practical aspects of running such a place. She knew how to order supplies in quantity, and who would deliver them without keeping too much for himself. She knew how to handle drunks, and, with the first women at La Paciencia, established a set of guidelines by which they would all live in order not to belittle or endanger one another.

Corona was more than happy to return to her place with the children, and Estela began to see that she must learn to judge just how much she could ask of a person before she was asking too much. Still, there was so much to do that she felt obligated to take on any task that was not yet spoken for, whether she knew how to do it or not.

"You must pace yourself," said La Señorita to Estela when she returned from the school one night. "Rome was not built in a day."

"Rome did not have trouble finding clean water."

"You must learn how to ask the right people," said La Señorita.

"What people? I have asked everyone, everywhere."

"The *right* people," said La Señorita. "I will show you tomorrow."

The next day, dressed in fine black lace, La Señorita marched into the mayoral offices and demanded to see the inspector for sanitation. With Estela by her side, she was ushered through a series of mahogany doors until they came to rest side by side in chairs before a massive desk. La Señorita proceeded to ask the man behind it, who appeared small in comparison to the desk, about his wife and children, whom she knew by name. Coffee was brought, and even candy.

After an hour of pleasantries, La Señorita declared that she was taking up much too much of the gentleman's time, and they left.

"What was that all about?" asked Estela when they were outside waiting for the carriage to be brought about.

"You wait and see," said La Señorita.

Sure enough, two days later, an aguador—oversized jar secured to his back by a strap across his forehead—appeared at La Paciencia bearing fresh water for the cistern. He appeared regularly, twice a week, after that time.

"How did you do that?" asked Estela, mystified. "You didn't even mention the water, or the school."

"When we left, the Minister immediately inquired as to what we might have wanted. Someone was sent out to discover the school and its needs. He was informed of the situation, and it was resolved."

"That's amazing," said Estela.

"You will soon be able to do that yourself," said La Señorita. "I am counting on it."

"But it is magic," Estela protested.

"Nonsense," said La Señorita. "Demeanor is everything."

✳

One evening just after she left, Estela's worst fears came true. The police came and arrested everyone at the school, including poor Corona. They were rounded up and carted off like common criminals. This was not new to some of the women, but to others, like Corona, it was a terrifying experience.

When Estela and La Señorita were able to sort it out, it was discovered that the women had been arrested as an illegal religious order, all of which had been outlawed during the War of the Reforms. While groups of nuns still maintained cloisters, certain palms were crossed with money so that, should a raid be planned, the women received enough notice to be gone when the police arrived. When La Señorita protested that these were, to the contrary, women who had been rescued from the streets, where they had lived emphatically secular lives, the officer in charge of the police activity admitted that the presence of children had momentarily confused him. He had deduced, however, that they were there to provide cover for the women.

With enough plata, the issue was resolved, and the women released. There were peals of laughter when the women were informed that they had been mistaken for nuns.

"Imagine," said Hermelinda. "And me with five children."

"I thought you had three," said Estela.

"The older two live with my sister in Tepotzlán," she said. "They help with the goats."

After that, plata was regularly paid to the police on the beat in their neighborhood, something that Estela had neglected to take care of among the many details of life in the Capital.

"Insurance," La Señorita called it. "It will be safer for all of you."

It was all too much for Corona, however, who returned to her mother's house and did not come back to the school for two months.

✳

During the Holy Week before Easter, the bells of the many churches were silent, and people carried matracas, noisemakers, to fill the void. Also during Lent, the women of La Paciencia, along with most of Mexico City, engaged in joking and banter to lighten the gravity of the air. Things were said in public that would not have been acceptable at other times of the year, from personal insults to limericks about politicians and religious leaders, and some were published anonymously in the papers. Often these took the form of an epitaph for Judas, but the living target of the barb was easily deduced.

The first year, Estela was scandalized by the things the women said to one another, but she soon came to realize that this form of wordplay was an art form in itself.

"Oiga, comadre, isn't that your husband's staff?"

"No, señora, if his staff had been that long, I would never have left him," came the response, followed by helpless laughter. This would go on for hours as the women washed clothes at the canal, or prepared food in street-side stalls. Woe to the man who made a remark to one of these women when she was armed with matracas! For unless he was equally prepared, she would cut him to shreds for all to see in public.

Estela came to see that, in a place where people had so little and lived so close together, humor, never her strong point, helped to lighten the load. She also saw the fear and superstition that was hidden just below the surface of everyday life—fear of losing one's three requests of Divine Providence, of losing one's children to disease or hunger, of incarceration, of being beaten and robbed for what little one had on this earth.

The matracas, wooden contraptions that were spun in the air to make a noisy rattle, were not only the toys of children, but a way of making oneself known to the invisible spirits, to scare off the devil and let the guardian angels know where you were. For the same reason, firecrackers were set off constantly, and images of Judas exploded in the poorer neighborhoods, often dressed as a landlord or a politician or some other target of revenge. The devil was thought to hover close during Holy Week, waiting for people to slip up during Lent so that they could be carried away on leathery wings to a place of eternal damnation.

Year-round, the broadsheets were full of stories of sons who murdered their parents for money, women who tortured children for the sheer pleasure of it, bandits who could not change their errant ways, despite numerous chances to repent. These people were all seen to be the playthings of the devil, and little monsters circled them, wild-eyed and ravenous, in the illustrations of their lurid deeds.

Although they seldom made it to the firing squad, these people were often condemned to death, a fate that was hotly debated among the upper classes. The existence of the death penalty in Mexico was seen as one more thing that separated it from the more refined judicial systems of Europe. The fact that the sentence was often commuted to hard labor was seen as the only mitigating factor allowing this system to continue. But a sentence to break rocks in the Valle Central was a fate almost as terrible as death.

Estela saw the joking and the fear, and saw how people with so little control over their own lives could wish so fervently for the favors of Fate and Divine Providence. And what was her fate? she thought, one afternoon when she should have concentrated on something else. To wait. To wait for a letter saying, Meet me Thursday afternoon. And although most of the time she pretended to herself not to care one way or the other about these letters, the arrival of one sent her into a frenzy of bathing and combing, of choosing her finest underclothes, and going at the appointed time to the little pensión just outside of the city, where the same room afforded, from a certain chair, a view of a tiny courtyard full of fruit trees. Estela came to cherish this view, one which she spent many hours contemplating, waiting. Sometimes he did not arrive at all, and Estela returned to her work silently, unfulfilled, yet not entirely ungrateful for the time alone.

When these letters came, the affairs of La Paciencia receded in size in her mind, shrinking down to a manageable level for just a few hours, when she was willing to say to Hermelinda or Corona, "That can wait." And it did, while Estela went to the pensión.

What was so different, Estela sometimes asked herself, between waiting in Saltillo for her absent husband, gone on some long and dangerous expedition, and waiting in Chapultepéc for Victor Carranza? That she did the latter by choice, she decided. And sometimes, if it did not suit her, she did not wait at all, but returned to La Paciencia, where new emergencies were sure to greet her.

One long afternoon, as the shadows reached across the mountains, and Popocatepetl smoked moodily in the distance, Estela composed a matraca herself.

Here lies Judas
He betrayed his Lord
He betrayed his wife
He betrayed his mistress
And he betrayed himself.

She knew that it was nonsense, but just the same, it made her feel better.

THE WELL OF SORROWS

Estela held her shawl wrapped tightly, her head and shoulders swathed in its dark folds, her face all but invisible. She hurried through the dirty streets, stepping across crying children, maimed beggars reaching out to grab her clothes, destitute women left to fend for themselves. Everywhere she looked, she saw hunger, she saw need. Mexico City seemed to her like a great stew of humanity, cooking in its own fetid juices. She clutched Noé's hand tightly, the boy silent as he tried to keep up with his mother's quick strides.

Deeper into the heart of the city she made her way, searching for the lane that would bring her solace. Turning past a display of baskets, a coffee vendor, dozens of faceless doorways secured with wrought-iron bars against the rabble of the streets, she approached a gate with a curious design and rapped furiously upon the latch.

"Open up!" she cried. "For the love of God, open up for your own blood!"

At first she was met only by silence, but by and by, long after any other petitioner would have given up the cause for lost and moved on to a more hospitable household, she heard a door open and close somewhere beyond the gate. Slow, shuffling footsteps approached and, after a further delay, a key was inserted into the far side of the gate. When it swung open, she could see a peaceful courtyard within. At its very center stood a low fountain, water spilling in a smooth sheet over its rounded lip, only occasionally ruffled by a breath of air. She stepped inside and sank gratefully to the warm flagstones, knowing she, or at least her son, was safe at last.

It had taken Estela a long time to find this place. She had asked and asked, receiving no definitive answers—only that they were here or there and they were safe, or probably safe if they were here or there—until she remembered the old scribe in the Plaza de Santo Domingo and wrote them a letter. It had taken many days, but eventually a letter had come back with an address in a colonia where Estela had never been. He had handed it to her with a twinkle in his eye. "Twice lucky," he had said.

Upon receiving it, Estela had flung some clothes in a bag and left without telling anyone where she was going or when, if ever, she would return.

"Noni," said Mariana into the face of the child in her arms. She repeated the word. "Noni."

Noé stared at her, then smiled and waved his hands so that she would say it again. Each pronouncement of the word was accompanied by a jog into the air for him, and it was difficult to say which he wanted repeated more, the word or the little ride.

Mariana and Julio had not seen Estela since before they left Saltillo over a year ago. And although Noé had been born, Zacarías' troubles had prevented them from seeing their only grandchild. Estela hardly had a chance to feed him as Mariana carried him around—showing him the treasures of her garden, the shape of an egg, the taste of sugar, then salt, on his bewildered tongue. On his own, Noé tasted the smooth tile floors, the loaned furniture, the earthy walls that now surrounded Julio and Mariana in their final exile in Mexico City.

His grandfather's eyesight had gradually faded the farther he got from Saltillo, as though his sight had remained behind, remained tied to the land of his birth. Julio went over his grandchild's face with his sensitive fingers, feeling the long, curved nose, the dark widow's peak that marked Noé as a Carabajál. The boy's tiny fingers, surprisingly strong, closed around one of his large ones. Julio, still able to distinguish between light and dark, held up a cut-glass crystal and flashed patterns on the wall. Noé seized the crystal and examined it before putting it in his mouth thoughtfully.

"And what does the future hold for you?" the old man asked him.

"Oh, stop it," said Mariana, taking the child from him. "The future holds everything for him. No more and no less. He will live into the next century, when we are dust."

Noé looked from one to the other of them as they spoke, his grandfather in a strong voice, his grandmother in a voice like wind sighing through trees, wondering what it could all mean.

Estela stayed in the spare room and wept. She threw herself on the bed and wept until no more tears were left, then she stared at the textured walls and felt sorry for herself. What had she been thinking, coming to Mexico City by herself? How could she have imagined that Victor still loved her, or had ever loved her? She felt the fool, dragging her child and her trunk with her, leaving all that she had ever known or loved behind.

All she had found were ruined women, abandoned children, shattered dreams, the empty dance of parlor politics. She could not bear the thought of making small talk with yet another patrón who may well have illegitimate children of his own on the streets. She could not understand how La Señorita could continue the way she did, her knowing smile bestowed on saint and scoundrel alike, her mind always one step closer to a solution for today's problems. But unlike herself she was born to it, Estela thought with a sigh, adjusting the wadded shawl under her cheek. Estela felt emotionally battered, wrecked upon the shore of her own ignorance and idealism.

No, it was not true. Victor had awakened her to her own true self. She had tasted love with Victor, even if he had not. Her love had grown, had become something bigger, something outside of herself, and it was her own love that she had followed, that had given her the courage to break with her past, with her sedate and pointless life, to follow him. Perhaps nothing good had come of her feelings for Victor Carranza, but she was a different woman than she had been before. She did not miss the old Estela.

Then why did she feel so bereft, so alone? She hated waking up by herself, knowing that Victor was in his wife's bed. She tried not to imagine them together, but sometimes the images were overwhelming. She had to fight the urge to send word that she must see him or go mad. It had been three weeks since she had heard from him.

Estela collapsed again into dry sobs.

"Mamá," said Noé as Mariana brought him into the room.

"He only wants his mamá," said Mariana, "not his noni. Especially when he is tired."

Estela sat up and took the toddler from Mariana, lifting him onto the rumpled bed. "What are you holding?" she asked, and Noé allowed her to unfold his hand, in which he was clutching a little straw man on a donkey.

Estela held the little figure up for him to see, then hid it behind her, pulling it out suddenly so that Noé laughed with pleasure. She did this over and over, scolding the little man until Noé begged to hold the toy, then handed it back to her to hide again. Estela felt her mood lighten, and gave herself over, for the time being, to delight in her son.

A few days later, Mariana, a wraithlike figure, emerged from the house into the garden. All in white, she was shrouded in the early-morning miasma that permeated the city—made of smoke from the cooking fires, an odiferous mist that resulted when the early-morning sun topped the mountains and fell upon the saturated streets and steaming, sometimes burning, piles of waste.

The old woman bore a tray of white crockery, arranged as if for breakfast. She made her way through the garden, past the murmuring fountain, to the far end of the walled enclosure. There, she had discovered an abandoned well with a single, shattered white cup at the bottom. The cup had looked so forlorn, its bones lying there on the damp sand, yet so free of its former uses and entanglements, that it had inspired Mariana to her own use for the well. She unceremoniously dumped the food-encrusted china off of her tray and into the dry well, where the cups and saucers, dishes and bowls shattered with a satisfying crash.

She sighed and straightened her shoulders, as though a great weight had been removed from them, and returned to the house. Mariana was still in her long nightgown, her gray hair loose over a white shawl draped around her shoulders.

The second time Mariana emerged from the house, she was followed by Estela, also in a nightgown. "What are you doing?" Estela asked.

Estela never knew if this was some odd custom or other passed down to her mother-in-law from her ancestors. Was it the Sabbath? Were they forbidden from washing dishes? Were the dishes unredeemably unclean in some theological sense of the word?

"Oh, this is something I came up with the second or third time the maid didn't show up," Mariana whispered in her papery voice. She paused a moment to allow Estela to catch up with her by the hostas. While Mariana's diminutive figure was able to hurry unimpeded down the twisting path, Estela had to part the tall pampas grasses and bend below the trailing branches of fruit trees to keep up.

Mariana proceeded to the well, where she set her tray on the mortared rock of its edge. "This house had a room full of china when we moved in. Years' and years' worth. It's so hard for me to heat the water and wash the dishes now," she said, showing Estela her arthritic hands, "that when Tula doesn't show up, I throw the dishes in here. I call this the Well of Sorrows," she said. Mariana picked up a teacup and held it out over the mouth of the well. "And I throw my sorrows into it. This is the avocado that went bad yesterday," she said, and dropped the teacup, which crashed to the bottom. "And this is the carriage that splashed mud over Julio when he finally ventured out for a walk." Crash.

Estela watched Mariana wide-eyed as she proceeded to name difficulties and drop dishes. Estela tentatively picked up a plate, then tossed it into the well, not naming her difficulty out loud. But Mariana seemed to sense its nature.

"And this," said Mariana, picking up the white china teapot, "is the trouble caused by men in general." She held the teapot by its handle and spout, caressing the spout with a surprisingly frank gesture. Then she dropped it with a glorious noise.

Estela gasped and covered her mouth. She had no idea that Mariana had a sense of humor, much less a ribald one.

"You know," said Mariana, "they say that man and woman together, when written in the old, sacred language, include God. But without God, they make fire and consume each other."

Mariana then picked up the now-empty tray and blessed Estela with a dazzling smile, and she, too, immediately felt better. They returned to the house together as the mists began to burn off, and Estela noticed the beauty of the lush green plants. This was a different climate than her native Saltillo, and she was often startled by the tropical quality of the vegetation. Tula, now arrived, opened the door for them and looked at the empty tray with dismay. Estela had not eaten in three days, but now, upon re-entering the kitchen, she realized that she was hungry.

Estela picked up her boy, who was playing on the floor with some peacock feathers, and kissed him and then dressed him in fresh clothes. She would wash her hair and return to La Paciencia, to see what joys or disasters awaited her. She knew that La Señorita must be frantic, must wonder if they were dead or alive. Perhaps she had even contacted Victor Carranza, to find out if he knew where they were. Good. That would make him worry, too.

Then Estela stopped herself. No. She would no longer think about him, would no longer care how he felt, good or bad. If she was to survive, she must put all thoughts of him out of her mind, must become as indifferent to his suffering as to his happiness. It did not matter whether he knew or not that she was missing. It did not matter whether or not he cared. Estela busied herself with dressing, with putting her things back in her bag, with covering Noé with kisses.

Mariana watched with approval but said nothing. When Estela was ready to leave, Mariana put a hand on her arm.

"Stay with us," she said. "Live here. Noé gives us new life."

Estela smiled and shook her head. "I have work to do," she said. "People need me." She stopped at the gate. "But we, Noé, will visit often," she said. "He needs you, too."

"Don't tell Julio that I told you this," said Mariana, leaning forward in a conspiratorial manner. Estela could barely hear her. "But you are a part of *tikkun lam*—the repair of the world. God uses many of us, even if we do not know it."

"Yes," said Estela, not really comprehending, but feeling somewhat repaired herself after her stay with the Caravals. "I suppose so."

As though suspecting that age-old secrets were being whispered by the women, Julio called loudly for Mariana from somewhere in the house. The abuela bestowed one last kiss on her nieto and shut the gate.

"Noni," said Noé, then collapsed with a sigh against his mother.

✳

She should have expected disaster to greet her. Upon entering the courtyard, Estela found several women pummeling one another and screaming. She grabbed a broom from a woman standing gape-mouthed in the corner, handed her bag and Noé's hand to her, and fought her way through the knot of bystanders egging them on.

"La directora! La directora!" they yelled, and all but two of the women stood back. When Estela managed to separate them, she found herself gazing into the eyes of a blind woman. She could not have been more than twenty. Except for her eyes, which smoldered like two burned-out coals, she was beautiful. She was fiercely clutching a chicken to the front of her tattered dress.

"What's going on here?" asked Estela. "I leave for a few days, and you all revert to lunatics!"

"We are just trying to take the chicken from her, señora," said Hermelinda, more mildly than her fierce expression would suggest. She brushed her hair out of her face, which was red with exertion. "She just joined us today, but she doesn't seem to understand that she cannot keep the chicken with her."

Estela patted Hermelinda on the arm, motioning for her to step back, then approached the blind woman where she crouched on the ground. When Estela touched her elbow, she flinched.

"I'm not going to hurt you," said Estela. "What is your name? Do you speak Spanish?"

The woman slowly raised her head and faced Estela's voice. "Eusabia," she said. "My name is Eusabia."

"Well, Eusabia, I am Estela. We will take care of you here, give you plenty to eat. So you don't have to worry about keeping that chicken. We will feed you."

"No!" screamed Eusabia, and doubled herself around the chicken. For the first time, Estela realized that the chicken might be alive, if barely. Eusabia rocked back and forth in a repetitive motion, holding the chicken close, as if it were her baby.

Estela took a chance. "What is the chicken's name?"

The other women, now standing around in a large circle, tittered and repeated the question to one another.

"Honoria," came the muffled reply.

"Honoria," Estela repeated. "We have a special place where we keep the chickens. They have their own house, here at the school. We feed them, too. We keep them only for eggs, which the women sell. When we eat pollo, we buy it from the market. Would you like to see where the chickens live, Eusabia?" Estela immediately regretted using the word *see,* but it did not seem to matter.

Eusabia raised her head again and slowly nodded. This time she allowed Estela to help her get up from the ground and retrieve her dirty bundle of clothes from where it had fallen in the struggle. Estela slowly led Eusabia back to the corral, where she was greeted by the clucking and whirring of the chickens, and the proud crowing of the single cock, standing atop the coop. For the first time, Honoria showed signs of life, and Estela placed Eusabia's hand in the grain bin so that she could feed the pet chicken. Eusabia smiled and sat down in the dust and feathers, where the chickens gathered around her like kindred spirits. And so Eusabia came to be the keeper of the fowl.

As Estela watched her there, she wondered how many teacups, how many plates and dishes, how many teapots would have to be cast down the Well of Sorrows to erase this woman's past. Then she wondered how much the plates and dishes could be sold for, but realized that they were not hers to sell, and so had no value for her. Estela shrugged and returned to the main courtyard as half a dozen women closed around her, enveloping her in their voices, each with a story to tell from the last few days.

L'ORCHESTRE TANGIER

I t was the contrabajo that pushed El Profesor Murillo over the edge.

"No! Absolutely not!" He threw down his baton and went outside, where he stood smoking and fuming until Estela came outside to mollify him.

"Profesor . . ." she began in a low, soothing voice.

"An audience simply will not stand for it!" he exploded. "Bad enough that we have women playing the cello. But the bass? No. It is simply a man's instrument."

"Now," said Estela carefully, "when we asked you to help us, you knew that it would be an all-female orchestra. And part of the appeal is that the women play *all* of the instruments. Hermelinda happens to play the guitarrón, which is like a bass. In fact, it *is* a bass, only held sideways. Why not a bass that supports itself on the floor? It is much easier on the back! And much more dignified in appearance. Please, Profesor. Come back inside and see what she can do. We need the low notes as well as the high, the bass as well as the treble, in order to be a full-fledged orchestra. These women need you!"

And so on, until her pleas wore the man down. He finished his cigarro and agreed to audition Hermelinda on the bass for L'Orchestre Tangier.

Now, this was no ordinary orchestra. Yes, it was all women, unheard of at the time in Mexico, though probably something that had already come and gone on the Continent. But these were no ordinary women. Rescued from the streets of Mexico

City, where they had sold songs and much more in order to feed themselves and their children, these were the beneficiaries of La Señorita Mejora's ministrations.

El Profesor Murillo had attended a soiree of La Señorita's one evening, in which the idea of women playing classical music in concert had come up. A journalist had insisted that women could not be taught the finer points of music and were fit only for folk melodies and lullabies. Caught up in the spirit of the conversation, El Profesor had bet the man that he could take women randomly selected from the street and train them to perform in concert. La Señorita had offered to find women worthy of the honor and, with Estela's help, had in short order assembled twenty women ranging in age from sixteen to fifty-eight whom they thought might fulfill El Profesor's expectations. If he won the bet, the orchestra itself would be the recipient of the rather generous purse to which the two men had agreed.

"It's always about men," confided La Señorita to Estela afterwards. "Even if they think they are talking or arguing about women, it is always about each other. We are simply a mirror of their boundless egos. Might as well put it to good use."

Not for the first time, Estela wondered at the circumstances that had allowed La Señorita Mejora to remain free of male entanglements, living in a spacious house with rich furnishings, owner of several ranchos and sugar refineries in the surrounding countryside that provided her with a generous income. Estela also wondered again how Dr. Carranza had come to know this woman, whose upper-class status and spotless reputation allowed her to give freely to the charities of her choice and entertain politicians and artists alike in her beautifully appointed salon.

"It is a small city," Carranza had said more than once, but Estela found it vaster and bleaker and grimmer than anyplace she had ever seen in her life, even more than the savage-infested expanses of open space surrounding her hometown of Saltillo. She had never gotten over her first few days alone in the city, beset on every side by beggars, thieves, and charlatans of every sort, some of them even well dressed. Not until she had been taken in as a boarder by La Señorita had she felt safe, felt that she could release her grip on her son Noé and lie down to sleep without fear of molestation.

La Señorita had relaxed that evening on a velvet settee and sipped a last glass of imported sherry as her maid cleared away the crystal and silver left by the other guests.

"We shall start an orchestra of women," declared La Señorita. "We shall provide gainful employment for these women, and prove that they can deploy themselves in a useful and decorous manner. What's more, people will pay to see them."

At that, a vision filled Estela's head, and she gasped. She realized what La Señorita was talking about. She meant to create a performing group, such as the many groups made up of men who played throughout the country, traveling from one fiesta to the next, following the saints' days and many holidays that formed a framework for the fabric of rural life.

"But where would they go? Where would they stay?" asked Estela. "Who would take care of their children and see that they were paid and not misused?" Her head was filled with a dozen questions. Estela had become much more practical in recent times.

"All in good time," said La Señorita tranquilly. "God will provide the answers."

And so L'Orchestre had begun. It was Estela, after she had overcome her initial shock at the idea, who had devised the name.

"It is French," she said. "And it is exotic."

Everyone agreed that this described their endeavor, embracing the foreign, somewhat risqué notion of an all-female orchestra.

It started with a few donated instruments, or instruments forfeited by men who had left them behind when they went off on drunken sprees.

"Perhaps," said La Señorita, "they will pay to visit their instruments again in a concert hall."

This led to much speculation about which instruments that the men possessed meant the most to them, or in some cases, were most missed by the women.

In any case, a few trumpets, guitars, and marracas were acquired in this manner, but the orchestra needed more European instruments if it was to pass itself off as something more than a ragged band of street performers. This led to Estela's second visit to Monte de Piedad.

Estela had dreaded going back. She sent Josefina on a regular basis to make payments on her mother's necklace, but she had been unable to face it herself. Each month, she imagined that a mistake had been made and the necklace sold off to some unworthy person. Estela imagined it around the neck of some vulgar courtesan, or between the fingers of a gross, uncouth man who had purchased it merely to adorn his mantelpiece. Thus, when she returned to the cavernlike interior of Monte de Piedad, accompanied by Josefina, she did not even look in the direction of the bright baubles and gems that taunted the poor who entered its premises every day. But Josefina made a beeline to it, even as Estela tried to pick her way between bulky sofas and silvery embossed saddles towards the area where musical instruments were for sale. Not a concertgoer herself, Estela was only vaguely aware of what she was supposed to be looking for, relying on descriptions repeated to her over and over again by El Profesor.

"¡Aquí está!" called Josefina. Estela turned to see her gesticulating at a glass case. She could not help herself, and made her way over to the case.

There it sat, as lovely as ever, its beauty barely dimmed by the insufficient light and tawdry atmosphere of the place. Estela feared to draw attention to the necklace, but those around them were intent on their own pursuits, their own dreams placed on temporary hold by the realities of day-to-day living. A woman walked by carrying a huge parrot in a cage, and Estela wondered if she planned to hock the bird, wondered how long it could survive without food or water amidst the flotsam and jetsam of people's belongings.

Estela sighed over the necklace, but lovely as it was, the idea of raising the money to redeem it was less appealing than it might have been even five months earlier. Next to it, Estela noticed a pearl necklace, so dewy that it appeared to be made of water. Even as she looked, a drop of water detached itself and fell, spreading a spot on the ragged piece of velvet below.

"Look at that!" she said to Josefina. "That necklace is dripping water!"

"It is lonely," said Josefina. "It weeps for its mistress, who will not redeem it from its prison. Who would rather be with the common people than among polite company, where she could wear the necklace to advantage."

Josefina did not approve of Estela's new life. Although she would remain faithful to the end, Estela knew, this was not the life she had bargained for in entering Estela's household—the life of a vagabond in rented rooms surrounded by women of dubious reputation. Josefina did not like Mexico City and yearned for her town in the north. She was not interested in lifting up the poor, only in keeping herself from becoming one of them. And in their present situation, it was difficult, at times, to draw the distinction.

"We will come back for it someday," said Estela. "My mother would have wanted me to do so."

Estela returned from her foray with two violins wrapped in a shawl and with a boy lugging the contrabasso. Josefina carried a flute, a little battered, but like the other instruments, with a story to tell.

✳

"Ah!" said the man, his eyes lighting up as though he had found a live one. "So you are starting an orchestra!"

Estela had entered his shop to inquire about the kettle drums in the window, which he was using as tables on which to display sarapes and jewelry.

"You want to start a real orchestra, such as one that might be found in the finest capitals of Europe?"

"Yes, yes," said Estela. "Exactly."

"Then come with me."

Estela summoned Josefina, who had remained standing outside, and the two of them followed the man as he exited the back of the shop and led them down a steep stairway. They then proceeded down a corridor the walls of which soon turned to bare stone, descending by inclined passages and irregular steps to a lower and lower level. As they made their way, Estela carefully lifting her skirts away from the damp walls and floors, the man kept up a running conversation.

"I happen to have in my possession one of the finest instruments to have made its way across the ocean."

He stopped to produce a large bundle of keys from his pocket and unlock a door before they proceeded further into what Estela was sure were the pre-Hispanic roots of the city.

"In fact," he said, "it is said to have been ordered from Hungary by the Emperor Maximiliano himself."

The man handed his torch to Estela and proceeded towards an area covered over in old, musty blankets. He began to pull these away and deposit them in a heap in a corner until a large, formless shape was revealed. The man then took back the torch and held it high to display his treasure.

At first Estela could not make out what she was looking at. Once she realized that it was very large, rather than the size of a violin or a trumpet, she found herself staring through the dimness at a hodgepodge of brass tubing and rosewood, of buttons and stops and pedals and gadgetry that culminated at the top in a set of pipes shaped into the spreading tail of a gigantic peacock.

"What is it?" she whispered.

"An orchestron," the man proudly announced. "It is a self-contained orchestra, one that can reproduce the sound of an entire orchestra with the labor of only one man. Would you like to hear it?"

Estela looked at Josefina, who had taken on the demeanor of a trapped animal, and nodded.

With a flourish, the man took out his handkerchief and dusted off the molded, leather-covered seat. He then sat down and proceeded to pull and push stops, ring bells and step on pedals, until the small space in which they stood was filled with the tolling and whining and pinging of a thousand voices, a thousand souls in the tortures of Purgatory, desperately singing the praises of the Lord in order to be released.

When he stopped and the ringing had abated from Estela's ears, she found Josefina collapsed on the floor in tears, her rebozo pulled tightly over her head.

"Please, no more," she sobbed.

"No, no more," said Estela as she helped her elderly servant to her feet. "That's all we will listen to."

But Estela had by now caught La Señorita's entrepreneur-ial spirit, and realized the potential draw of such an infernal machine.

"How much?" she asked.

The man named an exorbitant sum, enough to buy a fine house in an elegant neighborhood.

"Oh, no," said Estela, and turned to leave. She should have known better than to even ask, she thought.

"Wait, wait," he said. The man stood rubbing his elbows, as though the strain of producing those noises had somehow lodged in his bones.

"I'll tell you what. If you can pay for the services of a few men to move it out of here, I will give it to you. You see," he confessed, "my father received this contraption in lieu of a debt owed to him. But it is of no value now because no one wants it. An orchestron without an empire," he said, turning back to face the gleaming monstrosity, "is of no use to anyone. If you can put it to good use, then God bless your endeavors."

"Bueno," said Estela. "I will consult with my patrona, and we will send you word as to her decision."

Let us not go into the details of how an agreement was reached, or of how the services of six large, muscular men, the strongest that could be found, were contracted for one early morning in the market, or the subsequent injuries suffered by the men, the building, and the machine in extracting it from its stone catacomb. We won't dwell on the spectacle that ensued as the fabulous orchestron was carried through the nar-row streets of Mexico City, attracting a crowd of urchins who hooted and screamed and skittered before and after, of men and women who spoke for days of the event. And we certainly won't repeat the words that passed La Señorita's lips when the contraption finally arrived at her home and scraped off the molding at the carved entrance before it was deposited in the vast salon in which she intended to hold her concerts.

Once it was set in place, its bearers paid and off to find the nearest pulquería, it was clear that the orchestron was destined to spend its time on earth in that room, should the room outlast it. With dust rising from its many orifices and valves, its leather parts stretched and wheezing, the instrument almost seemed to exude the smoke of subterranean fires. One pipe was shaped into the head of a peacock, continuing the fantasy of the pipes rising behind it. On either side of this pipe were set glowing opals like eyes that seemed to stare at them malevolently.

"Done," said La Señorita. She eyed the giant mechanism as it crouched in her salon, trying to gauge the number of paying guests who could be accommodated around it. "Now we must find someone fit to play it. And I think I know just the one, or rather," she added mysteriously, "the two."

BLOOD AND CEREMONY

ne evening, when Estela returned, weary and hungry from her day at La Escuela de Paciencia, La Señorita had visitors in her parlor.

"Come join us," called La Señorita as Estela entered the front hallway and removed her hat.

"Good evening," she said as she entered the beautifully appointed room. It was decorated in red and a subdued indigo, which set off La Señorita's black-clad figure, elegantly reclined on a red settee. Next to her, on a table, was a large arrangement of red roses in a black vase with Chinese figures on it. Estela could not help but notice that the decor made her, perpetually in grey, look like part of the furniture. La Señorita's solicitor, Humberto, was there, along with another gentleman Estela did not recognize.

"Forgive me," she said, "but I would like to see my son for a moment."

"Here I am!" said Noé, and stood up from behind the settee where he had been hidden.

"Mamá," he said, and came forward for an embrace.

"It is too late for you," she scolded. "You should be in bed."

"Oh, let him stay just a little," said La Señorita. "I will have Carmela bring you some supper."

"Please, Mamá," he begged. "Señor Anslao was telling us about the bullfight!"

"Well," said Estela, sitting down and pulling Noé into her lap, where his feet dangled almost to the floor, "at least you are in your nightclothes."

"Go on," said Noé to Señor Anslao. "And then what happened?"

"And then again, he allowed the bull to pass so close to him that it practically creased his trousers. He did not even flinch. Did not even change expression."

"They say it is his Indian blood that allows him to remain so calm," said Humberto animatedly. "They say that he does not care if he lives or dies."

"If that were true," said La Señorita, "he would be dead by now."

"Only on the third pass," Anslao went on, "did he plunge the sword into the bull's back, as smooth as butter. The bull did not even buck. It looked up once, as though looking into his tormentor's eyes, questioning his fate, and slumped to the ground. The crowd was on its feet, throwing hats and cushions. They gave Ponciano two ears and a tail."

Estela had never attended a bullfight, but she had seen the bloody broadsheets that extolled the virtues of the matadors. Noé, of course, had seen them, too.

"And will Ponciano fight again soon?" asked Noé. "I would love to go."

"No," said Estela. "You are too young."

"Listen to your mamá," said Anslao, "not to the ravings of an old man." He looked up at Estela. "Don Porfírio, of course, does not approve of the bullfights, but allowed them to be reinstated because they are so popular with the masses."

"He disapproves so much that he is often there," said Humberto.

"Forgive me," said La Señorita. "This is La Viuda Quin-tanilla de Carabajál, director of the school. Estela, this is

Señor Enrique Anslao Gomez. He is an official in the Ministry of Justice."

Anslao rose and greeted Estela, who smiled politely. Carmela brought her dinner on a tray and set it to Estela's right on a low table. Noé slid to the floor to allow her to eat.

"Señor Anslao is a friend of mine from school," said Humberto. "We have known each other for many years."

"Yes," said Anslao, "and I am very interested in La Señorita's work with the women of the city. She tells us that you have been a godsend to her, that she could not do this work without you."

"I'm sure that she could," said Estela. "She was doing much before I arrived."

There was someone at the door, and a servant hurried to answer. Someone spoke, and although she could not hear what was said, Estela recognized his voice.

"It is time for you to go to bed," she said to Noé.

"But Mamá . . ."

"It is already late. You have had enough of a treat, and you have school tomorrow. Say good-night to everyone!"

Noé took his leave reluctantly. "Will you come back again?" he said to Anslao. "And tell more stories about the bravery of Ponciano?"

"Absolutely," said Anslao. "And other matadors as well."

"There will be other nights with more stories, we promise," said La Señorita with a smile.

"I will be there soon," Estela said to Noé, "to say good-night."

At the door to the parlor, the visitor said hello to him. The boy mumbled a greeting, already fading, before being led off to his room.

"Ah, Dr. Carranza!" said La Señorita, smiling brightly. She stood and welcomed him. "I believe you know Señor Anslao, Humberto, of course, and Señora Carabajál?"

"Yes," he said, nodding to all. "Hello." He sat in a chair near Estela, the coolness of the night air still fresh on his clothes.

"Hello, Doctor," said Anslao. "In fact, didn't I see you today? Wasn't that an amazing spectacle?"

"You attend the fights?" asked La Señorita.

Carranza shrugged and smiled. "Once in a while."

"Both sides are always full," said Anslao, "the side in the sun, and the side in the shade."

"We, as Mexicans, can't seem to get enough of this bloody spectacle," said Humberto, smiling. "I suspect that Señora Carabajál does not approve."

Estela smiled. "I think I understand the need for theater, for the pageantry of it. But I'm not sure that I understand the mania for bullfighting in particular."

"Even the señoritas from the best families attend," said Anslao. "Sometimes the matadors dedicate the bulls to them."

La Señorita tossed her head. "Then there are the matadors. The newspapers are as full of their exploits outside of the arena as in it."

"Yes, it is not clear which behave more poorly—those from Spain or those from Mexico," said Humberto. The men laughed. "Except for Ponciano, of course. Everyone knows that he is pure. He dedicates every bull to his mother."

"But really, it is the only sport which all—los de abajo y los de arriba—enjoy in common," said Anslao. "It is the great equalizer."

"What do you think, Doctor?" asked La Señorita.

Carranza finished lighting his pipe. "I think to miss it is to miss something . . . essentially . . . Mexican."

"Blood and ceremony," said Humberto.

"Yes, blood and ceremony," said Anslao. "Is that Spanish or Indian?"

"Both, clearly," said Carranza.

"Yes," agreed La Señorita. "But don't you think it makes the Europeans look down on us?"

"I see them looking down from the side in the shade!" said Anslao, and all laughed again. "No, really. They look down on Ponciano and his fans, because he fights in the Mexican style. The Europeans and the upper-class prefer Mazzantini, who is clean-shaven, and who kills *volapié*, by running at the bull. People get very heated over these differences."

"But how are we to better ourselves if this is how we spend our time?" asked Estela. "Why does our national pastime have to be a blood sport?"

"That is our national *public* pastime," said Humberto. This was followed by knowing chuckles from the men.

Estela did not understand, and looked to La Señorita, who was smiling broadly. "The bed, they say, is the opera of the poor."

Estela blushed.

"Well, the better of us, like yourself, spend our time more productively," said Anslao. "Please, I'm sorry I returned to that subject. Please tell us of your work."

"Well," said Estela, looking again at La Señorita, "we have about a dozen women living at the school right now. We also have their children, and a number of children without mothers, or mothers who are completely perdida." She looked sad for a moment, then sat up. "But La Señorita has had a wonderful idea, a wonderful way to train some of the women."

All looked to La Señorita, who had relaxed again along her divan. "Music, unlike bullfighting, to soothe the savage beast."

"You propose to teach them music?" asked Carranza. Estela had not dared to look directly at him since he had been seated.

"A Profesor Murillo has graciously offered to put together an orchestra, providing that we can find instruments for it."

"An orchestra? Do you think you have any women with the . . . aptitude?" asked Anslao.

"We are a very musical people," said La Señorita. "Everywhere I go, I hear people singing, playing music in the streets. Every fiesta is based as much in song as in spectacle."

"But an orchestra," said Anslao. "You mean of European music?"

"Certainly. El Profesor is convinced that this is a reasonable and beneficial endeavor. It teaches discipline and cooperation. The mere exposure to classical music should be an uplifting influence."

"My wife likes music," said Carranza. Estela stared at her hands.

"That is splendid!" said La Señorita. "She will have to attend our first concert! We shall start a list," said La Señorita, now addressing Estela, "of patrons of the musical arts."

"Yes," said Estela, "I will see to that. I think I am tired now," she said, standing, "and must say good-night." She smiled at everyone in the room, not daring to linger on Carranza, who had a bemused expression on his face.

"I am so pleased to have met you," said Anslao, jumping to his feet. "May you rest well."

"Good-night," said Estela.

"Good-night," said the others.

As she walked past Carranza, Estela saw his hand lift towards her from his lap, turning to expose the palm. She could not tell if it was a gesture of entreaty, or in response to the conversation around them.

Estela went up the stairs to bed, checking to see that Noé slept soundly. His room, next to hers, was light and airy. La Señorita had arranged to have a mural painted that went all around the upper walls, a foxhunt, with the fox hiding in a huge tree directly over the bed. Estela stepped over toy soldiers and horses to kiss the dark widow's peak on her son's forehead.

As Estela undressed and brushed out her hair, she realized that she had been completely tense from the moment Victor Carranza had entered the room. She was irritated with La Señorita, who would stay up late talking with the men, and with Victor Carranza, for mentioning his wife. He seemed so natural around her and other people, so cool, while she herself felt that, at any moment, they would be exposed. At the same time, she was upset that he did not try to acknowledge her once in any special way, unless that was what he was doing—the upturned hand, partly shielded from the others, as she passed. Estela could not be sure of this, as she had barely looked at him once.

Also, she was surprised to learn that he attended the bull-fights. He had never mentioned this. She brushed her hair more vigorously. He probably assumed, and assumed correctly, that she would not approve. She remembered the description of the matador, fearless in the face of death, as though he did not care whether he lived or died. Was she missing something essentially Mexican by not attending the bullfights? Estela decided that her life, at this point, was essentially Mexican enough.

Beautiful, strong, Rosalinda had shown up at La Paciencia one fine June day. She was dressed in blue and white, for from the age of twelve, she had dedicated herself to the Virgin Mary. Rosalinda was over six feet tall, and her sturdy frame could not be completely disguised by her modest attire. Her face glowed with good health and religious devotion, but she had no family. She had no place to go after her parents and siblings died of overwork in the cane fields owned by a rum producer southwest of the city. When they were buried, Rosalinda felt that she could no longer work there, and no one had the heart or strength to keep her from leaving.

Although most of the women who sought the shelter of La Paciencia could recite a litany of woes at the hands of men, Rosalinda appeared unscathed. She would have gladly joined one of the clandestine convents in the city tolerated by Don Porfírio and his wife, spending her days in meditation and hard work, but she had no one to offer a dowry on her behalf as a bride of the Church. Even under the stress of illegality, since the War of the Reforms, the convents would only accept women of a certain background, women whose families could pay with gold for the privileges of the spirit. Even the illustrious Sor Juana Inéz de la Cruz, before speaking too often and too loudly and too intelligently, had been allowed to wear the veil only after a wealthy patroness paid her dowry.

Rosalinda was not suited for domestic work or for teaching or caring for children. Her spirit, like her body, was large and restless and required strenuous activity. While Estela and Hermelinda struggled to find a place in the world for such a magnificent creature, Rosalinda was put to work repairing some of the masonry on the building. She would lower herself on ropes over the crumbling parapice, clutching her trowel, and three or four women would guide the rope, anchored at its far end to a massive stone urn, one of several that delineated the roofline. One of the less timid women would approach the edge and lower bricks to her with which to shore up the facade of the building.

Rosalinda also took on other tasks.

Often the former or abandoned or missing husband, lover, or procurer of one of the residents would come seeking his woman at La Paciencia, usually under the fortification of a great deal of pulque. Some of the men looked quite contrite, standing with head bowed and hat in hand, in hopes of showing their remorse. Sometimes they came with a child or two, and for this, the gate would at times be unlocked if the father was willing to relinquish his children to the care of the school. Others would rage at the portal, demanding that what was theirs by rights be returned to them.

One gentleman in particular had made a nuisance of himself, swearing and hurling accusations of the broadest sort at the locked gates, causing passersby in the street to stop and stare, and drawing undue attention to the school, which wished to maintain a low profile.

It was during one of his visits that Rosalinda was working above him on the facade of the building.

Infuriated by his foul language in the presence of women and children, Rosalinda pushed herself out from the wall against which she worked. This caused the urn above to begin edging slowly but inexorably towards the edge, and the women threw themselves against it and clutched at the rope in an effort to save Rosalinda from certain death. They held back the urn, but the bricks and mortar fell with a great deal of noise to the walkway below, barely missing Rosalinda and the rude petitioner at the gate.

As wrapped up in his own tirade as he was, the commotion caused the man to look up, where he was met by the sight of an avenging angel, swathed in billowing clouds of blue and white, and brandishing a trowel dripping mortar.

"Get away from here, you miserable man!" shrieked Rosalinda in a ringing voice. "Take yourself to a church and pray for the salvation of your soul, which I fear is in great danger of perishing from the evil that you cultivate within!"

The man took his hat and left in a great hurry, and was never seen again at the gates of La Escuela Paciencia. For all they knew, he was still praying, and still looking up. Rosalinda was given the nickname La Guardia, and at times when the elderly gatekeeper was met with an especially troublesome set of circumstances, Rosalinda was summoned to intervene. The repairs to the facade were never finished, but everyone agreed that it looked better than it had before. A simple board was hung over the gate which read EN SU CUIDA.

After some time, Rosalinda was apprenticed to a printer. She worked without pay for a long time, but finally one of the oldest men in the shop died, and Rosalinda was allowed to take a place at the end of the line, for one half the pay of the lowliest boys sweeping the floor while she set type.

"One half!" said Estela. "But how can they expect anyone to survive on that pittance? And of all people. Rosalinda is worth at least three of those skinny men picking away at those jobs."

"She is lucky to get paid at all," said Humberto. "Most bosses will not hire a woman for man's work."

Estela said nothing, only crossed her arms in a manner that she had. They had had this discussion before, many times, and no one would concede defeat. There had to be some way to educate the women about their rights, and the employers about the worth of women.

"Perhaps if we started our own publication," said La Señorita. "We need a way to reach more women. More than we can serve through La Paciencia."

"But most of them cannot read," sighed Estela, staring out the window.

"Pictures," said Hermelinda, who was present that day. "I have seen booklets that are just pictures that tell stories, or that can be used to tell a story."

"Yes," said Humberto. "There is a man from Pueblo who makes such engravings. They are marvelous."

"Who would make them for us?" asked Estela. "And how will we pay for them?" After all this time, Estela had learned the value of money. She paid all of the expenses of the school out of one of La Señorita's accounts, and was able to say to the penny what they had been in any given month.

"The ladies of the city will pay for a publication that suits their needs," said La Señorita. "I have seen such things in their houses—rules of etiquette, and so on. They are afraid to look foolish before their friends, and so they are slaves to anything or anyone who says she knows how to decorate for a party, or has the latest word from Europe. If we publish such a thing, they will buy it. And with the money that we collect this way, we will print up the picture books for women in need."

Estela looked at Hermelinda, who looked encouraged. Humberto smoked imperviously.

"Well, we can try," said Estela.

"Andale," said La Señorita.

They decided to name the magazine *Viajes,* for all of life is a journey. The first issue ran a story on buying linens in Italy, suggestions for a successful quinceñera, and an advice column from a priest for happy marriages. All of the columns were written by the women of La Escuela, dictated to Estela or Hermelinda, who, according to their judgment, would make suggestions on the contents. None of them had ever been to Italy, but Estela had celebrated quinceñeras with her daughters, and all of them felt that they could give advice as well as any priest, especially on marriage.

When it was ready, Estela took it to the Plaza de Santo Domingo, where each printer hawked the virtues of his press, the fineness of his papers, the neatness of his ink. A few also offered illustrations for the text, either his own or those that were readily available from nearby artisans. Estela walked up and down the narrow passages between the stalls, accompanied by Hermelinda, who borrowed Estela's umbrella at one point to fend off an especially aggressive salesman. Estela settled on one who didn't seem too difficult and left him with the copy.

When she returned in two days, he had two hundred copies of a booklet, with an engraving of an attractive woman on the cover, dressed as though prepared for a day in the country. Behind her stood a mozo with a docile horse at rein. Estela and Hermelinda took copies around to some of the bridal and millinery shops, where the shopkeepers were glad to place them in the windows, along with swatches of tulle and lace. They sold out immediately and merited a mention by one of the more well-known society columnists in the city. "*Viajes,*" he said, "is a treasure. It is something no well-brought-up woman can do without."

"That's good," said La Señorita upon being shown the column. "Especially the 'well-brought-up' part."

This quote was placed on the cover of the next issue, which included a feature on an attractive schoolteacher, including her illustrious pedigree, suggestions on cleaning linens from Italy, and an article on how to manage servants. This last had prompted a lively discussion among the women, who felt that the servants should be left to manage the household without interference from the mistress. Since only Estela and Hermelinda could read, Estela had adjusted the article to please its future readers.

Again, Estela took the handwritten copy to the printer in the Plaza de Santo Domingo, and this time she asked for five hundred copies. This was at the insistence of La Señorita, who, after all, was paying for it.

The cover art featured an attractive mistress standing with her hands on her hips, and before her stood two servants, a man and a woman, somehow smaller than she in stature. All three were smiling, although the servants looked respectfully at the señora's feet, while she gazed regally over their bowed heads.

"All she lacks," said Hermelinda as they studied the cover, "is to have her foot on one of their backs."

This issue of *Viajes,* too, sold out, prompting an editorial meeting.

"But now what shall we do?" asked Estela, in a panic. "I've put everything I know into the first two magazines. And then some."

Hermelinda merely shrugged.

"Don't worry," said La Señorita from her seat by the window. "I will give you information about the people of worth in the city. Now that we are so successful, we will accept submissions from our readers. People will be eager to have their name associated with *Viajes.*"

And so marriage notices were accepted for a fee, with long and elaborate descriptions of the wedding, the beauty of the bride, the bridal gown, the bridesmaids, and the party afterwards. The couple invariably honeymooned abroad.

Readers sent in their recipes for tamales, *marron glacé,* and other delicacies that took three cooks days and days to prepare. The lists of ingredients invariably called for items only available by import. There was religious poetry—always useful as a justification for purchasing the magazine—and tips on running an efficient household, given the deplorable training received by most domestics.

A schoolteacher in Puebla wrote to *Viajes,* convinced that this was an appropriate vehicle by which to encourage parents to teach their daughters to read and write. After all, a young woman who could not read could not write invitations or thank-you notes, and would have no idea who was calling on her on days when she and her mamá were receiving visitors.

Never mind that it took the whole family to decipher the magazine itself. Reading and discussing it had become a pastime that amused the entire city, and heated discussion took place over the merits of an education for young women. There were those who held that teaching women to read would merely expose them to corrupting ideas, while others actually called for women to be trained in professional occupations.

Most agreed that a certain amount of "finishing," preferably abroad, was good for a young woman, and helped to expend any excess energies that might remain from her childhood before settling down to the serious duties of wife- and motherhood. For this reason, even the most conservative among them approved of the magazine for its obvious Continental influences.

There were calls for the editor to make an appearance and defend his ideas in public. Invitations to soirees and dinner parties arrived every day. A name had been attached to the masthead—male of course—concocted at random from among the names and acquaintances within La Señorita's purview. It was finally decided to convey the word that the editor preferred not to appear in public. He suffered from some horrible, unnameable disfigurement, which caused him great pain to move about, and the editorship of *Viajes* was his only occupation and entertainment.

This caused a flurry of speculation on what the disfigurement might be, alternating with rumors that the editor was, in fact, a well-known journalist in the city who wished to remain anonymous. Neither idea was discouraged by La Señorita as she made her daily rounds of the best salons, gathering tidbits for the columns, noting novelties in dress, and sampling the best food that money could buy.

Another popular feature was fashion illustrations. The seamstress who was responsible for La Señorita's trademark costumes all in black was able to look at the wardrobes of the fashionable ladies as they passed in their carriages, or strolled in the parks reserved for those of better quality in the city, and copy them as "all the latest from Paris."

The patrona's seamstress described these imaginative dresses to a young woman from the country with obvious artistic talent. She had come from a large family of potters and had been charged with painting the designs that encircled the finished pieces. Upon talking to the seamstress, she had retired to the patio to work. When she returned, she carried several shards of pottery on which were illustrated the fashions. With nothing better to work from, Estela had taken these shards with her to the printer.

"What does this look like?" he said in exasperation, waving his arms around the open gallery where he worked. "An Etruscan mausoleum?"

Estela, who hadn't the faintest idea what such a place might look like, made no answer, but returned to La Paciencia with the pottery, careful not to smudge the designs.

The young woman, who really was very talented, was entreated to use paper. However, she had painted on a curved surface since childhood, and given a flat surface, all of the illustrations she produced were curved. Estela took these back to the printer, who erupted in gestures and loud mutterings once Estela and Hermelinda were out of earshot.

These sartorial designs were attributed to a Madame Plisser, and her trademark ruches and smockings were soon visible at all of the loftiest venues.

Because of its popularity with older ladies, who preferred not to have their reading contaminated by any of the more modern ideas of the day, the magazine soon became referred to as *Viejas,* and it was all Estela could do not to call it so in front of La Señorita, lest she take offense at her impertinence. Still, Estela suspected that very little escaped La Señorita, although never once was the alternate name mentioned between them.

THE FALLEN ANGELS

The father, a self-effacing schoolteacher, had first come to La Señorita upon hearing of her interest in "unfortunate women." He was the widowed father of two daughters who had fallen into wicked ways. Still, he was loathe to cast them out of his house, where they would surely engage in further depredations in order to fuel their great vice.

This case interested La Señorita for a number of reasons. First of all, it was almost unheard of for a man to take responsibility for the welfare of his daughters once they had become "desgraciadas." Secondly, these were not desperate, lower-class people such as those who usually sought out her beneficence, but decent, educated middle-class girls. Thirdly, the great vice of the two girls was not a wanton nature—though some of that had to be present—or drugs or alcohol, or even love. The daughters of Señor Pelegrino craved books. The father felt especially guilty because it was he who had conveyed to them by his own actions such an unnatural passion.

The señor had come to see La Señorita one sunny afternoon in her parlor. He was very shy, embarrassed at his situation, retiring by nature, and tended to mumble into the hat in his lap until La Señorita had the maid take it away from him. The man had taught for fifteen years and had been widowed for three.

"They were always perfect daughters," he said, "perfect." He had worried greatly when his wife died one winter of a fever, but the girls had accepted this tragedy with as much grace as could be expected. He had found it necessary to withdraw them from school, since, in paying off his wife's medical expenses, he could no longer afford the tuition. But since they were girls, it did not seem such a hardship. He had devised a course of self-education for them, which they eagerly accepted and followed faithfully.

As a schoolteacher, he drew a modest salary and provided for his motherless daughters the best that he was able. He was sober and tutored privately in the evenings in order to increase his meager income.

"It was these evenings, señorita," he said, that led to the first opportunities for temptation.

For while he listened to the p's and q's of a slow learner, or an adult learning to read for the first time, his daughters had begun to absent themselves more and more—first for twenty minutes or so, running one errand or another, then for longer and longer amounts of time. Yet when they were home, they attended to their chores and spent hours absorbed in books.

"Because they were always together, I thought that they were safe," he said. The man seemed momentarily overcome by emotion.

La Señorita nodded sympathetically. "Go on," she said.

This went on for several months until, to his horror, Señor Pelegrino was approached on the street by a man who inquired how much he charged for the services of his daughters. Upon confronting the two, they confessed that they had, indeed, been selling their bodies.

"They were doing this," said Pelegrino, nearly strangling on the words, "in order to buy books!"

La Señorita looked mystified. "But why? Weren't you providing these for their lessons?"

"They wanted more," he whispered hoarsely.

Graciela and Isabela, who were less than a year apart in age and greatly resembled each other, had, when freed of the constraints of the classroom, quickly mastered the rudiments of a classical education. They had gone on to master Greek and Latin, the French philosophers, and were, upon being discovered by their father, learning the mathematical theories behind astronomy. In order to obtain books, however, and not wanting to place an undue financial burden on their father, they had taken to seducing the scholarly gentlemen whom they encountered on the bookseller's premises. Rather than money, they preferred to be paid in books, drawing on the intellectual resources of their clients to locate and obtain the appropriate material for their studies.

When Señor Pelegrino had confronted his favorite bookseller, Señor Rodriguez de la Fuente, "a respectable man with daughters of his own," the man had confessed to patronizing the girls himself.

"They were so serious, he said"—Señor Pelegrino was wiping his eyes—"they were so serious and so beautiful when they asked, in exchange for books by Giordino Bruno and Johannes Keppler, one book each, that I could not help myself, he said!" At this point, Pelegrino dissolved into tears.

La Señorita had promised him that she would see what she could do. She was impressed but also a little irritated, because she knew the bookseller in question and had a taste for a small volume or two of poetry herself now and then. What was worse, although the girls had confessed to their father, they had been unable to break this vice, and still came home guiltily clutching large and valuable books, works their father could never afford to buy them from his modest earnings.

✸

Upon acquiring the orchestron, La Señorita had seen an opportunity. She directed Estela to pay a visit to the girls and see if they were suitable.

"If they are as beautiful and talented as their father says, then perhaps we can take this vice and turn it into a virtue."

Estela had never before visited the home of any of the women of La Paciencia, in part because most of them came to the school from the streets, or nearly so. So she was pleased to find herself calling at a boardinghouse that was more or less decent in nature, with a clean courtyard and a pleasant casera who showed her to the modest quarters of Señor Pelegrino and his two daughters.

Estela was indeed struck by the beauty of the two girls, nearly identical in appearance, with sparkling dark eyes and white teeth. They were, in fact, exquisite, and reminded Estela of her brother and sister, Membrillo and Manzana, who would always remain young to her. They had been twins, too perfect for this world, killed by a mob in Texas. But that is another story.

Señor Pelegrino anxiously showed Estela into his sitting room, clearing a space for her amidst the books and clothing that seemed to be strewn carelessly about. It appeared that the señor himself slept in the outer room, allowing the girls the privacy of the back bedroom.

"So," said Estela, somewhat at a loss as to where to begin, "tell me about yourselves."

"There is not much to say," said Isabela, the older. "We are average in every way."

"But that is not true," said Estela. "Your father says that you read Greek and Latin. That is very unusual, indeed."

"We have taught ourselves a mere fraction of what is possible," said Graciela after a glance at her sister. "And we hunger for more."

"So I understand," said Estela, with a look at Señor Pelegrino. "So perhaps we could help provide a way for you to continue your studies in a . . . legitimate fashion."

There was a moment of awkward silence, during which time Estela glanced around the crowded apartment. In a corner stood a covered jar for water, next to a smaller pitcher and sink on a narrow stand. Against one wall was a chest with a cloth over it, which probably doubled as a table. Near the window was a couch that clearly served as a bed, upon which Señor Pelegrino sat. The girls seemed content on the floor, modestly dressed and mannerly in their demeanor, while Estela occupied the only chair. Over the chest hung a painting on tin of Jesus showing his Sacred Heart, pierced with thorns and bleeding.

"You see how I feel about this," said Pelegrino as he watched her gaze fall on the icon. "Like that heart there, bleeding."

The girls hung their heads in remorse.

"But all is not lost," said Estela. "This is precisely why La Señorita started La Escuela de la Paciencia. She saw the waste of too many young lives, for want of an honest occupation. With your talents, she had something special in mind, and only wanted me to come and see if it might interest you."

The girls were intrigued. "Do tell us."

Estela went on to describe L'Orchestre Tangier, conducted by El Profesor, with its many and varied instruments and players.

"But for you," said Estela, warming to her subject, "La Señorita had in mind the opportunity to play the orchestron."

"Orchestron? Is that a type of instrument?"

"Indeed, it is. A very special one, which is able to reproduce the sounds of an entire European orchestra, all by itself. Now tell me, do you read music?"

"Yes," said Pelegrino. "They do read a bit. I have a violin, and they can both play and sing a bit."

"Then you should have no trouble in mastering this instrument, although it is very large and perhaps a bit complicated." Estela really had no idea what she was talking about at this point, but she continued. "But that should be no challenge to you."

The girls looked at each other, saying nothing for a bit. Estela felt her enthusiasm beginning to deflate. "But why is this preferable to what we have been doing?" asked Isabela. "Will it pay?"

"We hope so," said Estela, knowing that she could not fool these two. "We hope to give concerts in La Señorita's parlor, where the orchestron is situated. We will charge by subscription, and fine people will come to hear the music.

"You must understand," she went on, "that what you have been doing is very dangerous. Many women have come to La Paciencia who have been cruelly treated by men. They come with small children, lacking food or even basic clothing. You are extremely fortunate that your father has been so tolerant of your behavior."

"We tried making money other ways," said Graciela. "We made clothes for soldiers, and even baked bread and sold it downstairs in the courtyard for a while."

"But all of these occupations take too much time," added Isabela. "They did not leave us sufficient time for our studies."

"And what will you do with your studies?" asked Estela. She felt that she walked on unsteady ground.

The girls looked at her, then at their father. "We will know more," said Isabela, simply. "For us, that is sufficient."

"And what will you do when your dear papá has passed on?" asked Estela gently.

"We will teach. We will take all the knowledge that we have accumulated, and we will teach."

"In an accredited school, the teachers must be of good character," said Estela. "And I'm afraid that you have already given that away."

Pelegrino's face fell at that pronouncement. But an idea was coming to Estela. "But you could possibly teach at La Paciencia, where we all start out as equals."

Pelegrino looked up. "But aren't they too young?"

"How old are you?" asked Estela. They did look young, although they spoke well.

"I am fifteen," said Isabela. "And my sister just a little younger."

"Very well," said Estela. "Consider this. If you teach the women in the evenings, when they have returned from their jobs, you will have the days free to pursue your studies. But you must do so at La Paciencia, only returning home when your father is done with his own work. Unless, of course, you choose to live at La Paciencia. We can pay you to teach, enough with which to buy books. Only—" here Estela smiled conspiratorially—"we will keep your age a secret from the women, most of whom are older than you. Now," she said, rising, "I will leave you to discuss this with your father."

Pelegrino clasped Estela's hand with vigor as he escorted her out. "Thank you," he kept repeating in a low voice. "Thank you."

With La Señorita's agreement, Isabela and Graciela were engaged to teach at La Paciencia. Corona was greatly pleased to be relieved of some of her duties with the older women, since she had been teaching morning and evening and falling exhausted into bed each night. In addition, her temperament was better suited to working with children, and she was often left speechless by the questions posed to her by the women of the school.

At first the girls were appalled to learn that most of the women could neither read nor write. They soon devised a system, however, by which their students could apply the Socratic method of memorization in order to master the squiggles on the page and give them meaning. By constructing a house of memory—often based on a beloved, lost home or church—the women could attach a letter of the alphabet to the image of a concrete object, and so recall each letter upon visiting the memory. Rosalinda's house of memory consisted entirely of food from her childhood. Others used a park, or a place with some other pleasant association. Many used the premises of La Paciencia itself.

"I enter the door. Aquí esta la puerta. A. There is a bottle. Una bota. B," and so on, each woman reciting a different set of objects in a grand cacophony of noise that caused La Señorita to place her hands over her ears when she went to visit the class. And yet they learned, much to the relief of Isabela and Graciela, who were eager to move on to loftier subjects.

"Remember," said La Señorita, "that the women need practical skills. They are not going to become doctors or lawyers."

"What is more practical than being able to read and write?" asked Isabela. "Then the world is theirs."

Estela wished that she could be so sure. Many women had come through the doors of La Paciencia, and of those who stayed, many now had legitimate employment. At first Estela had thought that she could somehow save women whose lives had been destroyed by alcohol, but after a few years, she realized that the women who came through the doors, whatever their troubles, had to save themselves. La Paciencia was only a means to an end.

More troubling, however, were the increasing numbers of women who found themselves in desperate straits.

"Even as the rich build bigger houses," Estela said to La Señorita one evening at dinner, "more poor appear on the streets."

"It is no accident," said La Señorita. "The more the rich have, the less there is to go around. Don Porfírio's friends are very happy."

Noé followed this conversation closely. "But Los Cientificos say that education will solve all of our ills."

"Ah, Los Cientificos," said La Señorita with a dangerous intonation, turning to the boy. "All the problems of the world will be solved by logic. Is it logical for so few to own so much?"

Estela said nothing, only watched.

"If they are the capable ones," stammered Noé.

"And is it logical for so much of Mexico to be owned by foreigners?"

"They bring capital," Noé persisted. "And without capital, we cannot exploit our natural resources."

"*Exploit* is the key word," said La Señorita. "We exploit our resources, taking loans from foreigners to do so, exploiting our people as manual labor who do not share in the wealth. But one day, mind you, we will have to pay the bill." La Señorita was no longer addressing Noé, but some other, unseen audience. "The bill will come due, and we will pay it—in either money or blood."

"What would you have the country do?" asked Estela.

La Señorita shook her head. "I don't think there are any simple answers. We cannot be ruled just by the head, or by the heart, or by the Church as in old times. I would exercise caution in all things, but especially in making so much of our economy dependent on the goodwill of outsiders. The girls are right, you know," she said to Estela, "Isabela and Graciela. Education is the beginning of everything for the people of Mexico. But once the people know something, they will understand what they do not have."

Although she was not privy to the details, Estela knew that La Señorita had vast and complicated holdings, and wondered if she managed them according to her beliefs. If so, then she was managing her estate without an influx of foreign capital. Or perhaps with only a moderate amount. Estela decided that the latter was probably closer to the truth.

Glancing about the wood-paneled dining room, the finest of crystal laid out before them for a simple evening meal, Estela could not imagine La Señorita sacrificing her own comfort for the sake of ideals. Yet her work with La Escuela de la Paciencia was a contradiction to this, and she had once opened this very home to the unfortunate women of the streets. As in everything, La Señorita was a contradiction, a paradox, a conundrum.

A fter six weeks of practice, La Señorita announced that the orchestra was ready for its first concert.

"Impossible!" protested El Profesor. "We have barely scratched the surface of these pieces! You will make a laughingstock of us if you expose us to a concert audience at this point in rehearsals. You will make me a laughingstock of my colleagues if we do not have at least three more months!"

Seeing that El Profesor was taking this personally, La Señorita relented and granted them another month of rehearsals. The women redoubled their efforts, and much wailing and blatting could be heard coming from La Paciencia late at night as the women struggled individually to master their instruments. Many of them had taken advantage of Graciela and Isabela's lessons in mnemonic devices in order to commit the music to memory. In fact, most of them had learned the music by ear rather quickly; it was just the translation into sound—pleasing sounds, rather—that remained to be achieved.

In spite of his pleas for even more time, La Señorita scheduled a concert in the spacious front room of her home on April 24. Women studying to be seamstresses at the school had made costumes of white shirtwaists and dark skirts in the European style. La Señorita had insisted that the costumes be modest so as not to distract the audience from the high-minded purpose of the evening. Only Rosalinda, who had volunteered to play the percussion instruments, was allowed to retain her costume of blue and white. Engraved invitations were printed and sent to women who were known to buy *Viajes* on a regular basis, or rather, to their husbands and the señoras to whom they were married.

On the evening of the twenty-fourth, thirty-four couples in their finest evening wear gathered at the home of La Señorita. Many were there out of sheer curiosity, since her home was often the gathering place for intellectuals and politicians, but seldom a location for a purely social event. Among the guests was the gentleman, a critic and professor of music at the Lyceo de México, who had insisted that women could not be trained to play in such a manner. He looked worried, probably concerned that he might be forced to concede loss of his bet.

Each couple was greeted at the door by a uniformed butler, who relieved them of their wraps, then offered champagne and caviar on iced platters. Afterwards, they were shown into the salon, where comfortable chairs had been arranged in semicircles facing a raised dais. El Profesor, in a tuxedo, was kept pacing and smoking in a back room until the last minute, when La Señorita beckoned him out to greet the audience. She applauded as he took the stage, and the audience took its cue from her.

"Welcome," El Profesor began. He was very nervous. "Tonight, for your entertainment and edification, we offer two orchestral pieces. The first is a waltz by Viennese composer Johann Strauss."

He turned his back to the audience and raised his baton. He made a few tiny triangles in the air, establishing the time, as the women of L'Orchestre gazed up at him with fear and hope in their faces. Upon letting the baton fall, a noise emerged, not quite clear, but yes, as the audience listened, a melody emerged. At first it was faint, as each woman hoped the one next to her would cover her mistakes, then stronger and stronger as they gained confidence. It was not exactly Viennese in nature, but it was, in fact, a waltz.

The audience watched in rapt wonder. They could not take their eyes from Rosalinda, who towered over the rest in her white veil and vivid blue cassock. She banged the drums sturdily, and the professor had to push towards the floor with his left hand to convey the softness that he needed. Hermelinda, too, drew attention where she stood behind the bass.

The end of the piece was reached with much emphasis on the last four chords, and El Profesor turned to the audience, red and perspiring, but smiling. The audience broke into applause, and La Señorita, from her vantage at one side, silently breathed a sigh of relief.

Estela waited in the back room, where she and Corona had made sure that the women were dressed and coifed in a proper manner. Some of them had never put their hair up on their heads before, and in spite of the washing and brushing that had occupied the better part of a day, it had been a difficult task to make the women presentable. Not all of them were wearing shoes, but Estela hoped that their long skirts would cover this fact.

"Remember," Estela had said to the women before sending them out, "demeanor is everything."

Corona stood looking through the slightly open door, and Estela watched her, listening for reactions. The applause left her relieved, too.

A short intermission followed, during which costumes and hair were repaired, and El Profesor admonished or praised various members of the orchestra. During this time, the audience was plied with more champagne.

The second piece, by the Russian Modeste Moussorgsky, was in several parts. It was a little longer and more difficult to follow, and at least one member of the audience began to doze.

Estela heard a murmur beginning to rise from the group, and looked to Corona where she stood at the door. Corona began to gesture for her to look. Peering through the narrow gap of the door, Estela could see the orchestron presiding over the far corner of the room, on the other side of El Profesor. Puffs of smoke were issuing from the openings at the tops of the pipes, and she could have sworn that the eyes of the stylized bird had begun to glow with an infernal light. She wondered if it had caught fire, and tried to think where she could find a bucket if she needed to douse the thing.

Unaware of the cause of the stir, El Profesor cast nervous glances over his shoulder at the crowd. The women of L'Orchestre, as though mesmerized by fear, stoically played on.

Upon the completion of the piece, all roused themselves for further applause, and there was even one shout of brava! There were calls for an encore, and El Profesor had a surprise for La Señorita, one he had been preparing all along.

He nodded to her that the orchestra, which had remained seated, was prepared for an encore, and she assumed that one of the earlier pieces would be repeated. Instead, El Profesor struck up a Mexican melody, eliciting gasps of pleasure from the audience. The second time the chorus was played, people began to sing, and soon much of the audience was singing along with the orchestra. The conclusion was met with thunderous applause, during which El Profesor brought La Señorita to the front, where she stood and beamed, occasionally turning and gesturing to the women of the orchestra. At a signal from the professor, the women rose and left as one body. La Señorita had given strict instructions on this point. They were not to stay and risk any conversation with the guests, lest the refined veneer created by the performance be shattered by the reality of the untutored women.

"Now," she said as the last of the women filed out, "I hope that you see this as the tiniest example of the accomplishments of the women at La Escuela de la Paciencia. As you can see, they have worked hard to acquire the patience and discipline needed to perform such a concerted effort. In addition, many of them have learned other disciplines as well, such as tailoring and printing, so that they may go out into the world and support themselves in a decent and respectable manner. It is now up to you, good citizens, to make sure that positions are available to these women, and we hope that you will contribute generously to our efforts before you leave tonight."

The professor of music, Profesor Escovedo, rose to his feet.

"If you will allow me, dear lady," he said including the entire room in his address, "I think it is my place to acknowledge defeat. El Profesor Murillo has taken these unformed, uneducated women from all walks of life and transformed them into an exemplar of civilization. Let me be the first to contribute to your cause by paying off my debt." All applauded.

"It is not I," said El Profesor, stepping forward, "it is not I who have transformed these women, but the ennobling power of music. We have brought them to worship at the Temple of Minerva, to acquire a taste for knowledge and beauty in its highest form, and they have responded to her calling."

"And," said La Señorita, "the women themselves have wrought this transformation, with the help of a few. Please bring Estela," she said to Corona, who now stood in the doorway through which the women had disappeared.

Estela was just seeing the women and their instruments safely into an open carriage when Corona came out for her. She joined La Señorita and the professor in the salon, dazzled by the lights and applause, not sure what had been said. She kept her eyes on the floor as they adjusted to the bright room, the warmth and noise sweeping over and around her. Happiness suffused her, bringing color to her cheeks.

The hour being late, people began to rise and go. Half a dozen servants stood in the entranceway holding hats and wraps. They had been instructed not to relinquish these, however, nor call the carriages, until the owners had deposited money in the large glass bowl that had been strategically placed on a small table before them. Upon seeing the situation, the guests made their contributions to La Paciencia—some cheerfully, others less so—and ransomed their coats.

"We have not seen you at La Señorita's other gatherings," Profesor Escovedo said to Estela. "Where has she been hiding you?"

Estela looked away from the man holding her wrist. "I work long hours, señor, and usually do not partake of evening entertainments. Tonight," she said, looking at La Señorita and El Profesor, "was an exception, in that it involved the women directly." She noticed that La Señorita was wearing a ruby the size of a small house at her throat.

"You would be a welcome and decorative addition to her soirees."

Estela smiled and directed her gaze across the man's shoulder at a woman who looked familiar. La Señorita, who had been talking with other guests, stepped towards the woman and led her, along with an elderly woman, to Estela.

"I would like you to meet la Viuda Carabajál, the director of La Paciencia. Estela, this is one of our finest supporters, la Señora León de Carranza, and her mother, la Viuda León."

As Estela curtsied, she realized that this was Victor Carranza's wife, and felt a cold dampness upon her upper lip.

"I have heard so much about you," said the woman. "You are the woman in grey."

"Oh? Well, I guess I am," said Estela. She finally dared look
at the woman for a moment. La Señora Carranza was tall and
fair, her mother haughty and handsome even in her late years.
Estela's heart sank when she saw how beautiful Victor's wife
was. She smiled weakly, having nothing more to say, and hoped
that her cheeks were not aflame.

"Yes," said La Señorita. "That is how you are known among
the society women, as the Woman in Grey—for your dress, of
course, but also for your understated manner. Did you not
know that? I have told everyone how invaluable you have been
to me. Señora Carranza is very interested in our efforts. As is,
of course, her husband, Dr. Carranza, who volunteers his services for us. By the way, where is the doctor this evening?"

"I'm so sorry, he was called away to the bedside of a patient,"
said Señora Carranza. "A frequent hazard of a doctor's life,
I'm afraid. That is why my mother joined me tonight."

"Well, we are happy to be graced by her presence. I hope you
enjoyed the concert, señora?" La Señorita addressed the older
woman. Estela noted the gleam of heavy jewelry at her neck.
It put her in mind of her own mother's necklace, which she had
redeemed, then pawned again since her first visit to El Monte.

"It was very interesting," said the woman. "Very interesting
indeed. But is the performance of music, which will put them
in public view, a suitable alternative for these women?" she
asked. "After all, isn't the point to remove these women from
the, from the . . . public realm?"

Estela finally spoke up. "Some of them are just young girls
recently arrived from the country," she said. "Innocent and
unspoiled. In any event, we hope to uplift the whole person.
If their heads and hearts are not engaged, how can we just
train their hands?"

"I had their moral uplift in mind," replied the woman.

"That is the point of the entire school," said La Señorita. "That is why it is named after the Virgin, that she might serve as an example to all of them."

"Many of the women have become very pious, some going as far as to dedicate their lives to the Virgin," said Estela. "In any case, we have emphasized sobriety and propriety as a condition for staying at La Paciencia."

"We are so glad to hear that," said la Señora Carranza, who had become bored and distracted from the conversation, looking about to see who else might be present. "But we must go now, so that I can see my children into their beds."

The rest of the evening, in spite of La Señorita's unqualified praise, passed in a blur for Estela.

✱

Despite La Señorita's public plea, not a single job offer came to the women of La Paciencia in the weeks following the concert. La Señorita was on the point of engaging a manager to take the group on tour, despite the logistical nightmare posed by a group of women traveling in the countryside, when she received a visit from the owner of the Tivolí de Eliseo, the second roller rink to open in the Capital.

"We are proposing a new program at the Tivolí," said the man, "and one of my assistants brought your group to my attention."

"Go on," said La Señorita.

"We have had requests to set aside a few hours for women only, so that they may learn to skate without the distractions and embarrassments of the opposite sex. It would please us greatly if L'Orchestre Tangier would play during those hours, and so make the women further at ease."

"That sounds wonderful," said La Señorita. "And what would the hours and pay be?"

"We would like to hold the hours between ten and four on Sundays, opening the rink after that time to gentlemen as well. If that time is suitable, can we arrange for payment on a weekly basis?"

"Those hours would be appropriate, since some of the women have other employment. Please arrange for the amount of payment with my solicitor, Don Humberto. It will, I presume, be in keeping with the prevailing wages paid for such entertainment?"

"Oh yes," said the entrepreneur. "My colleague at the other Tivolí has had great success with its program exclusively for women, and we expect to do likewise. Exercise is all the rage, señorita, even among those who formerly disapproved of such things for women. It is seen as a healthy activity, both for the mind and the body."

"Andele," said La Señorita. "We are certainly in favor of that."

At last, La Señorita's experiment with L'Orchestre seemed vindicated. "The world is changing," she said to Estela. "And maybe Mexico won't be left too far behind."

Estela, only vaguely aware of the wide world outside of Mexico, did not know. "Maybe he would like to buy the orchestron," she said.

"That was an amazing effect during the concert," said La Señorita. "Although I'm not sure that it was not hazardous. How was that accomplished?"

"Do you think it was on purpose?" asked Estela. "I was ready to douse it."

"We will have to ask the professor," said La Señorita, "although he has never shown any affinity for it."

"I don't think he knew about it."

"Ah," said La Señorita. "Just as well."

The proprietor of the Tivolí came back to look over the orchestron. "I think not," he said finally, after inspecting the machine. "There is something sinister about it. Already, our American visitors object to our holding hours on Sunday."

"Why is that?" asked Estela.

"Well, the Protestants only attend church on Sunday, and so feel that we, too, should do the same."

"But Mass is said several times a day, every day of the week, all over the city."

"Still, it is their custom, and we need to attract foreign dollars when possible. The Americans may not skate on Sunday, when L'Orchestre would perform, but the orchestron would be there all the time."

La Señorita was disappointed. The orchestron took up a large portion of her salon and cast a dark and gloomy atmosphere over her once-cheerful gatherings.

"Ah well," she said. "Perhaps we can still find someone willing to perform on it."

"If business continues at the current rate," said the man from the Tivolí, "perhaps I will reconsider."

"Bueno," said La Señorita. "Until next time."

LA LINTERNA

One day La Señorita called Estela into her study. "It is time to launch our second publication," she announced. "*Viajes* has been more than a success and will support our efforts."

With her was a small, dark woman, smaller than La Señorita. Her feet barely touched the ground where she sat in one of the upholstered chairs. She set down her teacup and smiled brightly at Estela, not rising. Humberto was comfortable in his accustomed place behind a large desk, turned at an angle to the window to afford him a view of both the room and the garden, where the birds had been placed in their cages for air.

"This is Gloria Quinque," said La Señorita, "and I have asked her to be the editor of our new magazine. This will be the one for the real women, the working women of Mexico, who carry it and all its inhabitants on their backs."

Gloria, it turned out, was from Mérida, with an education at the famous school for girls La Siempreviva, founded by Rita Cetina Gutiérrez. Gloria herself had taught school in the villages until the authorities had forbade her to re-enter her classroom. Her students had acquired too many ideas about freedom and their place in the world, and the owners of the fincas had complained that they did not make good workers. Worse, there were other schoolteachers like her, and they met, when they could, on a regular basis. Since then, she had worked on publications sponsored by the parent organization of La Siempreviva.

Even given everything Estela had heard from La Señorita and her like-minded friends in Mexico City, Gloria Quinque had very radical ideas. It was obvious that she and La Señorita had been talking for some time before Estela was summoned—perhaps the sort of interview she, herself, had undergone some years earlier.

"Circumstances," said La Señorita, "are very bad now in the provinces. In the Yucatán, people are being mistreated on a scale never seen before, forced to work on the henequen plantations as slave labor. The recent international demand for henequen to bind wheat harvested with McCormick reapers has made the plantation owners rich and even more avaricious. The poor from all over Mexico, especially the rural indigenous, are being transported to the Yucatán. La Siempreviva has been working to counter this terrible trend."

"The henequen kings are worse than the conquistadores, who merely killed people," added Gloria. "Worse than the Aztecs, who, after all, merely ate people. The plantation owners say that people can only hear through their backs."

Estela shuddered at the imagery evoked by her blunt language. "What about the Church in the Yucatán?" she asked. "Aren't the Church fathers doing anything about this?" Estela found it difficult to believe that atrocities on this scale were being tolerated. She had heard of people being sent to the hennequin plantations to work, but always assumed that they were from the criminal element in the city.

"The Church merely promises treasures in heaven," said Gloria. "It does not promise what we are due in this life, nor does it show people how to attain it. Only the rich and the Church benefit from the present order."

A brief silence fell on the group, filled only by the singing of birds.

"Those who can, run away. And they come here, to Mexico City," said La Señorita. "They need to have hope for the future, for the future of their children. We can help."

A variety of provocative and inflammatory names—including *La Lengua, La Llorona, La Malinche*—were considered for the new publication. They also toyed with the idea of having no title at all, merely using individual, tantalizing words to begin each pamphlet. In the end, it was decided to use a more conservative name, *La Linterna*. They hoped to cast light into the dark corners of these women's lives, to give them light by which to see their way to a better life. Don Humberto waxed so enthusiastic on this subject that he was charged with writing an introduction to the first issue.

"But make it brief," said La Señorita. "Not all of this legalistic talk."

After much discussion, it was agreed that the magazine should take the form of brochures that would be primarily pictorial in content, with as little print as possible. The topic of the first pamphlet would be healthy children. Part of this, of course, was healthy mothers—mothers without too many children to feed. Leticia, a partera who was known to have done considerable business in the district of El Niño Perdido, was sent for.

"The women need to know where to go to see real doctors," she said.

"Aren't those working the streets examined every month by the Ministry of Health?" asked Estela.

"Only those who are officially licensed," said Leticia, "which is a fraction of the actual number of women selling their bodies. And those who are examined," she continued, "are given ratings: pretty, very pretty, and ugly."

Humberto suppressed a smile as he turned away.

"In spite of the promise of treatment for those who are ill, only those near death are detained and placed in the hospital."

"Where the authorities won't have to go out and collect the bodies," added Humberto, now sobered.

"They need to know how to take care of their babies," continued Leticia. "Away from their homes in the country, they don't have their abuelas and parteras to help them. Many of the women give their children pulque to drink, because they have nothing else. The pulque takes away the hunger."

"But we cannot change the order of things," said Estela. "How can we help all of the poor to find enough food? How can we educate all of them? Find them decent jobs and houses? We are just—" She motioned around the comfortable room at the people in it. "We are just us!" She felt overwhelmed by the proposition.

"We cannot change the order of things," said Gloria, "but we can change their place in it. They will have to change the order themselves."

It was also decided that future issues would cover such topics as labor organizing, where to obtain food and services for the poor who were newly arrived in the city, health advice, and perhaps, as a light note, a column on music by the Profesor.

La Señorita insisted that Estela turn to Victor Carranza for help.

It had been over a year since Victor had last sent word to Estela, and she had not seen him in the interim. Perhaps, she speculated, his wife had put two and two together after meeting her at La Señorita's benefit. Or perhaps it was his own choice. She was too busy, she had told herself, to worry about it. Nonetheless, she could never pass the little pensión on the outskirts of the city, or even the neighborhood, without it bringing back the taste of roses, mixed with the essence of her

own pungent desire for Victor Carranza. In any case, she did
not want to be the one to contact him.

"He's the only man," said La Señorita, "who will give honest
information to these women. Ask him to draw you the pictures."

"With the new Civil Code of 1884, this effort is more necessary than ever," said Gloria Quinque. "Now that we are *imbe-
cilitas sexus*, imbeciles by reason of our sex, we must do what
we can to help women survive on what scraps are left to them
by these so-called legal reformers."

Estela was also embarrassed by the material she would be
showing him. In spite of her exposure to the more sordid
aspects of life in Mexico City, and in spite of understanding the
need for educating the women, these were things that she had
been brought up not to discuss, or even acknowledge. Estela
suspected, at times, that La Señorita took pleasure in Estela's
discomfort with the earthier side of affairs at La Paciencia.
Nevertheless, she penned a professionally cool summons to
"My esteemed Dr. Carranza."

✴

After a month of work, Gloria came to La Señorita with a
mockup of the first pamphlet. La Señorita looked over the contents, and they decided to show it to the women in residence at
La Paciencia. They found it extremely interesting and began
to share their own experiences in such matters.

"The partera who delivered my babies knows everything
about babies except how to start them."

"Maybe she knows better. Maybe she knows how to not
start them."

"Eat something hot ahead of time."

"No, eat something cold, to cool him off."

"Eat a pickle. It works every time."

"Andale. And here you are six little pickles later. No, mujer,
put a pickle inside of you ahead of time. *That* always works."

"Mentiras. If he is strong enough, nothing will stop the baby."

"Or ugly enough."

"Sí, de veras. If the man is so ugly, he makes a big impression on the woman. And the baby will come out to look exactly like him!"

The text was adjusted accordingly, taking into account the terms the women understood, and the aspects of the subject that interested them.

"But this must remain a secret between us," said La Señorita, "or the authorities will cart us away to Belem, the penitentiary."

They all laughed, but there was a distinct feeling among them—Estela and Humberto, Leticia and Gloria—that their activities would be greatly frowned upon by the authorities in question. This was more than charity they were offering, thought Estela. This was revolution.

"We, together," said Gloria, holding her arms out melodramatically, "will be the new Malinche, the Tongue, and speak those things that have been forbidden to women: the knowledge of herbs and their beneficial uses that have been forgotten, the abilities of women to nurture the health of their own bodies, and to diagnose and treat the ills of their children. Above all, women need to acquire knowledge and learn to think for themselves."

"Brava!" shouted Humberto, and they all cheered.

Estela asked for the information as best she could, armed with the crude terminology of the parteras. Her own background and natural reluctance to discuss such things with a man, or anyone, was a great hindrance, but Carranza, when he finally responded, insisted that he was eager to help in any way that he could.

"I'm sorry that I have been so busy, cariña," he said, placing a hand on Estela's arm where they sat in the tearoom of the Casa de Azulejos, "but in the last few months, the number of

my patients has increased dramatically. People are bringing in
new and rare diseases from abroad."

Estela tried not to look at him. When she did, she found that
she could not hear what he was saying. So she kept her eyes
downcast and stuck to the business at hand.

The more that *La Linterna* took shape, the more they realized
that it was a dangerous proposition.

"We will need a different printer for this one," said La Señorita,
once she looked over the final copy that Gloria handed her.
"This has to be a special person, someone who will publish
our work without comment or prejudice. Someone who will
faithfully render and execute even ideas with which he doesn't
necessarily agree. Someone who can be discreet."

It was rumored that somewhere, in a certain quarter of the
city, such a printer existed. Descended from printers of Bibles
trained in medieval Italy, he was said to practice the ancient
craft on a press that was hundreds of years old, brought to the
New World by his ancestors. The press was said to be so small
that it could be folded up and spirited away on a moment's
notice, which accounted, in part, for the printer's ability to
appear and disappear like a migratory bird. M Cardoz only took
jobs that suited him, that he found to be of great societal or
artistic merit, and charged very little for his time and services.

His shop, supposedly, could only be found by those who
knew how to find it. It was open six days a week but invisible
on the seventh. And sometimes the shop was there, sometimes
it was not: It was not merely closed, it disappeared altogether.
When it was there, it was always open, but it could never be
found on Saturday, and rumor had it that M Cardoz, whoever
he was, observed the Jewish Sabbath. No one knew what the
M stood for. Estela, with her family connections, was instructed
to find this remarkable man, and was determined to do so.

After several fruitless attempts to find the shop on her own, winding through the tortured, narrow streets that surround the Plaza de Santo Domingo, where she had come to be a familiar sight, Estela went to her mother-in-law, Mariana, who sent Julio out, blind on the streets, to ask of the right people where the shop of M Cardoz could be found. Julio was known in their neighborhood, and a child soon guided the old man to a nearby building, one that he visited often, where other old men could be found drinking té de canela and discussing the intricacies of The Law.

Only ten were allowed to be on the premises at a time, due to the strict laws against unapproved assembly imposed by Don Porfírio, and so one man stepped out the back door as Julio was led inside, and took the opportunity to smoke while he waited for a space to become available, without calling undue attention to the assembly within.

When Julio returned after a while with the information, it was understood that Estela alone was to bring material for *La Linterna,* bearing the good name of her in-laws as a password. It was also understood that, although his shop could sometimes be found late on Fridays, where he toiled on his press within, he would not accept new commissions at that hour.

The shop turned out not to be near the Plaza de Santo Domingo at all, where the other printers were located, but rather nearer to the house where Julio and Mariana lived.

The first time Estela found the printer, he had set up shop in what was little more than an alley between two buildings. The name M CARDOZ was painted on a sign that hung at the entrance to the alley. She walked down the alley, which appeared to be a dead end, only to turn a slight corner and find a little shed that stood between the two larger edifices. M Cardoz stood as though waiting for her, his hands folded before him.

A few proofs were pinned to the walls of the shop, a few tools were scattered about, and a stack of paper filled the back of the small room. Estela was struck by Cardoz' self-contained nature. In order to attract and keep customers, the printers of Santo Domingo tended to be loud and aggressive. Cardoz, in contrast, listened quietly while Estela described *La Linterna* to him. When she finished, he stood for a moment regarding his press, which resembled something that belonged in a horse stable. She was almost certain that he was prepared to refuse the job.

"Like the *Tacuinum Sanitatis*," he said at last.

"Pardon?"

"The *Tacuinum Sanitatis* was one of the first books published by my ancestors in Soncino, Italy. It was a medieval health book, with illustrations, based on a text in Arabic called the *Taqwim al-sihhah*, by Ibn Butlan, written in about 1068. It served much the same purpose as you describe—to convey information on health and sanitation to an essentially illiterate populace."

Estela did not know what to say. "I thought the first book published was the Bible. In Germany."

"It was certainly the first book published in Germany. But shortly after, printed books began to appear in the Netherlands, Italy, and elsewhere. In Italy, *La Commedia di dante alleghieri* was soon published, along with many other works of drama and poetry. A little later, Chaucer's work was published in England." He smiled. "But that was only after he read the stories of Bocaccio."

Estela looked at her hands. "I'm sorry, señor, but my knowledge of literature is very shallow."

"It doesn't matter," said M Cardoz. "I was merely trying to show you that the endeavor which you propose has a long and

noble history. *La Linterna* is a very worthy project, and I will
be happy to take it."

*

Estela had to stop each time at the house of her in-laws in order
to discover the whereabouts of the mysterious shop. So Mariana
was gladdened because Estela would sometimes leave Noé
with his grandparents while she did her somewhat vague business with the mysterious printer.

Noé watched as his grandfather passed his hands over the
flame of the candle—once, twice, seven times. As he did so,
Noé's eyes grew dim to all but the sight of Don Julio, who
himself was now sightless. A whiteness now obscured the old
man's eyes, a permanent film of clouds from too much gazing
into the distance where he had no business, as a mere mortal,
to look.

Noé made himself a secure nest in the corner of his grandfather's study. But perhaps *study* was too strong of a word for
this austere room, for it held little more than a chair, a few candles, and a large table behind which his grandfather spent most
of his days. Most of Julio's books and Cabalistic paraphernalia
lia had perished in the terrible fire that destroyed the familial
home in Saltillo, and his sight had begun to dim almost immediately afterwards. It was as though, deprived of his precious
writings, he had found no reason to continue seeing.

At almost the same time, at the beginning of their flight to
Mexico City, Noé's grandmother, mute since childhood, had
regained her voice. And although it remained paper thin and
whispery, like the rubbing of insect wings on a summer morning, she was able to communicate to Julio by sitting very close
to him and whispering in his ear. This is how the boy often
found his grandparents, seated in the kitchen or by the great,
squat fountain that held down the center of their tiny courtyard,

flowers blooming in pots all around them. Sights, gossip, inspiration, and love made their way from her lips to his ear. Finding them this way, Noé felt as though he were intruding on a larger drama, as though Mariana narrated the turning of the spheres to her husband, not daring to raise her voice and disrupt the performance. And yet the boy was never turned away, but welcomed to them with open arms, café con leche and biscochitos soon warming his belly.

There was much that Noé did not understand about his family. There were things that his mother would not tell him about his father, Zacarías, whom he did not remember. There were things that she did not know, or understand. He sensed a combination of love and frustration when she talked about him. But most confusing of all was what had happened to his father. Whenever Noé asked, his mother said that she did not know— that Zacarías had gone off to the north when the authorities were looking for him, and that it was best not to talk about him in front of other people.

When he asked his grandparents, however, Noé received a different answer. Inevitably, his grandmother's face would light up and she would say, "Zacarías was called away to serve our Lord."

Noé wondered what that meant: to serve our Lord. He knew what a servant was. There was a woman who did all the washing at the house he and his mother shared with La Señorita Mejora. There was a girl who came in and cleaned his grandparents' house and cooked for them. These were servants, people who made their living by doing work that other people were incapable of or indisposed to do for themselves.

But did God need his house cleaned and his clothes washed? Noé had attended services at the Catedral with his mother, and God seemed to have lots of people serving him. Noé imagined his father doing laundry at a stream in the mountains. Whenever he thought of his father, Noé imagined him in the mountains to the north, laboring beside a tributary to the Rio Grande.

If his father was a servant, maybe that was why his mother thought it prudent not to talk about him in front of others. His mother emphasized to him the importance of class in Mexico City, where people judged you by the clothes you wore and the company you kept. She insisted that he attend a prestigious school and dress properly, and "comport yourself like a gentleman," whatever that meant. Yet she herself dressed simply and spent most of her time with the poorest of the poor, the working women of Mexico.

Julio recited the prayers and meditations that he had long since learned by heart, and after listening to him, Noé knew them by sound as well. But he did not understand them, and this bothered him. Sometimes, when his grandfather seemed to be in this world, Noé asked him, and Julio would launch into this or that reb's commentary on this book or that of the Cabala. Just as often, however, his grandfather would turn his milky-white eyes on him and say, "The older I get, the less I know."

But Noé continued to watch and listen, and save everything in his heart.

✴

At first Estela met the doctor in public places, conscious of other eyes upon them. But soon the meetings in hotel lobbies turned to an afternoon in a café, a long carriage ride, or a visit to the hidden pensión.

Each time this occurred, Estela was determined, afterwards, that it would not happen again. But each time, the doctor's quiet persistence led to the passionate caresses that they exchanged in a dreamworld of denial. As La Viuda Carabajál, there were no expectations that Estela maintain a public social life. She was free to concentrate on her charitable work for La Señorita, and it was assumed that she passed most of her evenings in pious meditation, or attending to the moral instruction of her young son. Or so she hoped.

Besides her qualms on her own behalf, Estela feared that the women of La Paciencia would discover her secret, and she did not wish to set a bad example. If she, a respectable widow, was found to be engaging in immoral behavior, not even for the purpose of procreation, what was to prevent these poor unfortunate creatures from returning to their former lives on the squalid back streets of the city?

Estela began to manifest the nervous habit of removing her gloves and twisting them between her fingers, as though wringing the neck of a small animal.

Carranza made sure, however, that Estela returned to the sunny parlor of La Señorita with new drawings, accompanied by simple explanations of their meaning. Leticia inevitably changed the wording of these captions to the popular terminology that the women would understand, and there was much lively debate over the relative nobility of this language, versus how demeaning to the dignity of women the more vulgar terms might be. Estela learned a great deal, both from the writing of the pamphlets and from the tender, personal ministrations of the doctor himself. Carranza was a very good artist.

This went on for some time, the doctor in heaven, Estela in denial, until the day that Estela and Noé encountered La Princesa.

✶

After the legitimate success of *Viajes,* the women of La Paciencia were not prepared for the notoriety that greeted *La Linterna.* While the publication was a popular success, selling briskly wherever it was offered, a copy, apparently, fell into the hands of a member of the officially sanctioned press.

CORRUPTING INFLUENCE IN THE CAPITAL, trumpeted a headline. WOMEN EXPOSED TO PERNICIOUS INFLUENCES. The article went on to denounce the contents of *La Linterna,* as "encouraging vice and depravity among the lower classes." Every copy was soon sold, and additional print runs were needed. The women of La Paciencia were warned to keep quiet about the publication's origins, every article being written under a pseudonym. Every bundle of magazines passed through several sets of hands before becoming available on the street.

Rumors were soon rampant that an obscure Masonic sect was working to undermine the moral authority of the Church. These people were said to be of either Dutch or English origins, and the British consulate went as far as to issue a statement denying all knowledge of the publication and its supporters. La Señorita did nothing to dampen these speculations.

Upper-class Mexicans were at a loss as to what attitude to take towards *La Linterna.* On the one hand, it was shockingly frank in its treatment of the female body. On the other hand, in a country that worshiped all things European, it was said to have a European influence. Soon, women from the more respectable families were sending their maids out to find copies, and most were well-worn by the time they reached the mistress of the house. There, she would retire to her boudoir with a headache and a copy of *La Linterna,* leaving strict orders not to be disturbed.

LA PRINCESA

I t was one of the endless number of special holidays called by Don Porfírio—the celebration of the birth of his child, the removal of his bunion, the continuation of his earlier administration, which had been temporarily interrupted by the puppet presidency of his dear friend . . . what was the name? Estela could not be bothered to keep track of such things. This must be in support of his reelection, she decided.

Circumstances had gone well for La Paciencia, and the publication of *Viajes* had funded four issues of *La Linterna* over the course of four years. Still, Estela had not become at home in Mexico City but was accustomed to it, as one becomes accustomed to a spouse, or a lingering cough.

Noé had grown to be an introspective twelve-year-old and Estela had enrolled him in a private school since the age of eight, where he could be taught Latin, Greek, and other disciplines essential for the life of a gentleman. Estela had few expenses, since she lived and dined with La Señorita or with the women at La Paciencia, and so could afford the tuition for her last son.

Once Noé began at the liceo, Estela could not help but think often of her oldest, Gabriel, and how his education had gone to waste. He had thrown it all away to become a heretic and a Protestant minister, even taking an Indian wife of illegitimate birth.

I am surrounded by heretics, thought Estela one day, when her thoughts were especially unkind. But this, she decided, was her due as a fallen woman. She had continued to see Victor Carranza, in spite of the misgivings in her heart. There was always a good reason for it, on behalf of the women of La Paciencia, and he either provided free medical treatment for the women or referred them to someone who would.

He even told them that there was a woman being trained as a traditional medical doctor, in spite of the protests of the professors at the medical school. This was of great excitement to the women who published *La Linterna,* as both an inspiration and a practical necessity that was long overdue. She needed the work, she had told the magistrate, to support herself and her widowed mother. Until then, women had left the country in order to receive medical training in all but its most ancient manifestations—birth, herbal and ritual curing, and death.

✷

So it happened that Noé was with her on the day of Don Porfírio's latest holiday, standing dutifully on El Paseo de la Reforma. His classes had been canceled in celebration of something that required Don Porfírio to ride by on a horse. When he did this, Don Porfírio needed an audience, and so the people of Mexico were required to suspend commerce and education and cleaning and cooking in order to witness this equestrian splendor. The event was accompanied by lavishly attired officers and a marching band in the European tradition and general hoopla, so most people did not mind.

Estela stood sedately, idly noting that Noé could use a new jacket, when she noticed his intense concentration. Noé could concentrate ferociously on the smallest object, turning his full attention on an insect, or a mosaic fountain, or the song of a water carrier. And he could be filled with endless questions or speculations on the object or event for days afterwards.

But when Estela followed his gaze on this particular day, she found him fixated, rooted to the spot, by the visage of a girl.

At first Estela found this amusing. The girl was dressed in a pink and white striped dress with a matching parasol, and looked as though she belonged in the window of a confectionery shop. She wore tiny, pink, high button shoes, which she stamped impatiently. Estela's vision of the girl was only occasionally clear through the crowd, and she wondered that Noé had even noticed her. But when a large number of people or soldiers or officials passed down El Paseo between them, Noé did not remove his gaze from the vicinity of the señorita. Estela began to wonder, after a time, if she was witness to the manifestation of an infatuation.

At last El Presidente made his appearance, to the deafening approval of the people on all sides. The sound grew louder and louder as he grew closer, like a wave roaring towards the shore. Estela rattled her fan noisily, as she had been instructed by La Señorita to do on such occasions. As the noise reached a crescendo, El Presidente swept by on his horse, surrounded by soldiers and statesmen and others of importance, at least in this life. Estela caught a glimpse of uniform and flashing gold buttons, a white-gloved hand held high in the air. Immediately upon his passing, the crowd began to lose interest and disperse, even as the seasons change from summer to winter with a breath of cold wind.

Just as Estela placed her hand on Noé's shoulder to lead him away, a woman placed her hand on the shoulder of the little girl in pink opposite them. The woman carried a snow-white, silk parasol of the finest quality. She was accompanied by a handsome man in a fine coat who could be no other than Victor Carranza.

Estela's heart stopped beating momentarily, but in the instant she had noticed them, they were gone. Noé unfixed his gaze from the far side of the street and followed his mother silently.

Estela employed her fan vigorously. "Did you know that little girl?" asked Estela when she was able to speak.

"La Princesa," said Noé, and Estela did not know what that meant—if it was a title he had invented on the spot or had heard from another. She did not have the personal resources, at that moment, to find out.

✳

As they walked home through the deepening dusk, candles began to appear in the crowd—at first a few, then more and more. Estela began to understand that this was a continuation of the earlier parade, but now taken on by the common people.

Estela stopped one of the candle-bearers to ask why they were marching.

"Los farolitos," answered the woman, "the little candles are in support of Don Porfírio, to show that we want him to continue in office as El Presidente. Because if he leaves, what will become of us?"

What has become of us now, thought Estela silently as the crowd flowed around them, that we are so dependent on one person, like a child on his father? She recalled a comment she had heard repeated a month or so earlier: "The good dictator is such a rare species of animal that the nation which has one should prolong his power as long as possible, even for life."

The isolated, flickering candles turned to a steady river of light, and continued to pour through the streets of Mexico in a continuous stream, thousands of marchers now, walking in solemn procession. The dim light was accompanied by the shuffle of bare feet and sandals, the occasional cry of an infant, the glint of candlelight off of a bracelet or earring. Almost all of the marchers were los de abajo, yet for once, they possessed a dignity that seemed to lift them above their circumstances. Many of the men were dressed in the simple white garb of the countryside, a style of dress supposedly banned from the Centro, but Estela noted that the policemen who stood along the route, still at their stations from the earlier parade, did nothing to apprehend them.

Estela, caught up and carried along by the crowd, experienced a profound sense of being at one with many people. It was both reassuring and frightening that she could surrender her will so easily to the masses. Noé clung to her hand wordlessly as they were swept along by the nearly silent people.

Don Porfírio's reign must be the will of the people, thought Estela, the will that is so respected by La Señorita's friends. But are we such sheep? That woman is right, she thought suddenly. What will happen when he is gone, if we so fear any change at all? It was not her place to know, but it filled her with a sudden dread of the future. There are so many people who have so little, she thought. What will happen if they are not united by a common will, governed by a strong personality?

Estela, still holding Noé's hand, continued silently in the crowd until she came to her street, where they struggled to free themselves and return home. The sudden darkness, away from the crowd, made them feel profoundly alone, and they entered La Señorita's house grateful for the cheerful lights within.

That night Estela could not sleep and did not rise in time to see Noé off to his classes. La Señorita remarked on the dark circles under her eyes at breakfast, something she did not usually do, so Estela knew that her agitation showed on her face. She moved through the day in a fog, and the next and the next, until it was time again to see Dr. Carranza.

He sent a carriage for her as usual, and met her in the pensión with a trustworthy innkeeper on the southwest outskirts of the city. She disembarked from the carriage and was shown to their room, a familiar place with luxurious green drapery and a view of a tiny courtyard.

Carranza arrived an hour later. When she saw him, Estela burst into tears.

"I'm so sorry I'm late," he said, holding her head cradled against his chest as she cried. "But someone came in who needed immediate attention." He continued to talk, apologizing and describing his busy schedule.

Just like a man, thought Estela, completely absorbed in his own world. "It isn't that," she managed to say.

"Then what? What is it, my life?"

"La Princesa!" said Estela, and Carranza looked at her, mystified.

"La Princesa?"

"Your daughter! We saw her at the parade!"

"Ah yes, Matilda! She is as beautiful as a princess!" said Carranza, and he beamed. "Where were you? I did not see you."

"With my son. Noé. He noticed her."

"Does he know her? She's just a child."

"So is he. But he called her La Princesa."

"Ah," said the doctor, as though he understood, but he wasn't entirely sure that he did. He sat quietly as Estela dried her eyes.

"Why does my daughter trouble you?" he finally asked.

"Because you have a family, a real family," Estela managed to choke out. "And I don't!" That sounded selfish and wrong, and wasn't what she had meant to say.

"Yes, I am very fortunate," said Carranza. Neither spoke for a moment, but both felt the hurt between them—of walks never taken, of friends in common they would never have, of meals they would never share, quiet beds, and old age.

"I feel," Estela finally pushed out, "that I cannot see you anymore."

"But why?" asked Carranza.

"It is not right. I mean," said Estela, determined to finish out this idea, "that I cannot continue to do this to your daughter and, and . . ." She could not bring herself to say it.

"My wife," Carranza finished for her. He stood and began to pace around the room. "Yes, my wife. What can I tell you about her? You saw that she is beautiful. She is from an old family, and we have known each other since we were very young. Before I was a doctor."

Estela was not sure that she wanted to hear this, but she had started them down this path.

"My feelings for her are different from my feelings for you. I guess I justify my actions," he sighed, pausing by the window and leaning on the sill, "because my feelings are so different that I don't feel that one interferes with the other."

"In other words," said Estela, "because I do not threaten your marriage." Her voice was low and grating.

"Yes," he said, "that is one way of putting it. But also, because I am not the only one."

"The only what?" she asked, honestly confused.

"The only man in Mexico with two women."

This infuriated Estela. "Don't I know that?" she said, rising up. "Don't I see their castoffs every day?"

"Please be calm," he said. "Please, let us discuss this as two adults, without letting other things get in the way."

Carranza walked around the room, agitated. He knew that he had said the wrong thing.

Estela sank back onto the bed, her head in her hands. She had not thought that her misery of the last few days could grow any greater.

"I know I should be grateful for my situation, for my association with La Señorita and La Paciencia," she said finally. "I am not in the same situation as those women, since I can earn an honest living. And I am. But I still feel that I should no longer see you. For your princesa, and for my son. Oh, what if he knew?" she suddenly cried out. "What if he knew what sort of a woman I really am?" She looked up at him, her eyes huge, her face streaked with tears.

Carranza put his arms around her but said nothing. They sat like that for a long time, until the warmth of his body began to soak the chill out of Estela's heart.

✶

Noé thought about La Princesa, the little girl whom he had named the first time he saw her. He had seen her once before, also during a holiday. She had been dressed in yellow, looking like a little bird that had just flown in from the countryside.

All of his life, Noé had played with the children at La Paciencia, poor children with little idea about life except to get enough to eat. But they had been full of games that could be played with nothing, a string and a rock, and his mother had not discouraged him from these transient friendships.

At the liceo, Noé had met boys from the better families, and soon learned not to talk much about his own. He was not sure why, but he knew that the situation of himself and his mother was unusual. There were two or three boys who were, nevertheless, sympathetic to him, boys who liked books and science and could argue at length about a single idea.

But La Princesa was entirely different. She stirred feelings in him that he had never known before. He wanted to protect her and build her a beautiful house. He wanted to ride on horseback with her through the park and tell her some of the things that he knew about plants. He imagined her standing on the high parapet of the great stone house that he would build for her, like the castle at Chapultepec Park, the sun shining on her pretty hair as he rode towards the house on a beautiful horse. That is why he thought of her as La Princesa.

✶

After four months, Victor sent word to Estela again, and in spite of her misgivings, she went to meet him. The absence had renewed their appetite for each other, and it was a long time before they truly spoke. And then, as though it was the most natural thing in the world, Victor Carranza remarked upon the birth of a son to his wife.

"Why didn't you tell me before?" she asked.

"I thought you knew," said Carranza, as if his life were published in a bulletin every day. "I have never tried to hide anything from you." He sounded peeved.

Estela realized that, by questioning their relationship, she had placed it on a different footing, and it was not a happy one.

"That does it," she said. "One day your son is going to see this old woman on the street, and his friend is going to nudge him and say, 'That's your old man's mistress.'"

Carranza said nothing. She saw by the way that he moved his shoulders, turned his head so as not to look at her, that he was restless, embarrassed by her outburst.

Walking to the window and looking out, he said, "You will always be beautiful to me. As beautiful as the first day I saw you in Saltillo, turning your foot in the street." And he smiled at the memory.

Estela went and stood behind him, putting her arms around him and pressing her cheek against his back. She tried to recall the times, long ago, when she was oblivious to what other people thought. She remembered how reckless they had been, as though they had been invisible. She was grateful for happy memories of the past. A slight breeze entered the window and stirred the single rose in the vase on the table, causing the edges of the petals to quiver like the lips of a lover.

BRINGING DOWN THE CLOUDS

Estela sat in the courtyard of La Paciencia fanning herself against the hot night. The city groaned and grumbled around her like an unhappy giant, and she was afraid to go home, afraid to leave the women of La Paciencia to their own devices on an evil night such as this. The city was in the third year of a terrible drought and most of the residents were subsisting on pulque, but even this was beginning to run out as the maguey plants themselves began to die of thirst, the water tables dropping below the reach of their deep, enduring roots.

She wasn't sure what she thought might happen. Both Hermelinda and El Profesor had been missing for three days, and she suspected that they were together. She was both furious at them—for neglecting their duties to the school—and worried that misfortune had befallen them. Several of the women had not yet returned from their jobs, were long overdue, and Estela was loathe to lock them out as midnight approached.

One woman came up to the gate and waited resentfully as it was unlocked.

"Where have you been?" said Estela. "You should have been back ages ago."

"Are you my mother?" the woman shot back before making her way to her room. She might have been inebriated.

More and more, the women who had collapsed gratefully at the gates of La Paciencia had come to resent the restrictions imposed on them. Mindful of the protection provided by the strictures, they had come with their children to escape abusive husbands and lovers, to see their children fed and clothed. Some had come with sores and contusions, with infections that required the attention of a doctor. Their children limp with malnutrition, the women had surrendered them to the ministrations of Estela and her helpers.

Yet some of the women had been mistresses of their own time, unused to the rigorous schedule at the school. A few left immediately upon regaining their strength. Others left when it was made clear that they were expected to work in some capacity, either within the school or at a respectable occupation outside of it. Some had come and gone several times. Estela, per La Señorita's instructions, never turned them away, as long as they were sober within the gates of the school and did not fight with the other residents. Some moved on but left their children. Sunday afternoons were reserved for visits between these families, and Estela was able to see their hopes and fears played out—children waiting impatiently for the impending visits, or for the mother who never returned.

Estela could hear the dogs barking from the city dump, a horrible, wild noise of fear and gluttony. Somewhere a donkey brayed, vehemently, and stopped short, or was stopped, mid-breath. It made her shudder and pull her shawl, which had fallen down around her elbows, a little closer.

The stars above the courtyard were hard and bright, and Estela could hear the creak and clop of a carriage coming through the streets long before it came to a halt before the school. Even before the gatekeeper had let her in, Estela recognized the small black bundle as La Señorita.

"Why are you staying here?" she asked, motioning at the women sitting and dozing, or talking in small groups around them.

"I . . . don't know. I'm worried. Hermelinda is gone."

"And the professor?"

"Yes."

"Well then," said La Señorita with a dismissive wave of her hand, "let them be gone. They'll come back."

"Is Noé asleep?" asked Estela. She had sent him home earlier with Josefina.

"Yes, he is fine. But you must not preoccupy yourself all the time with these weak women," said La Señorita. "Leave it. Come with me. I have something to show you."

"Oh, no," said Estela. "I'm too tired to go anywhere."

"This will take no energy," said La Señorita, taking Estela by the arm and steering her towards the carriage. "This will give you reason to carry on."

The carriage dropped them at the train station, and without a further word passing between them, the driver tipped his hat to La Señorita and drove off.

La Señorita boarded the southbound train with Estela, greeting the conductor as though she knew him well.

"Where are we going at this hour?" asked Estela. "I have no hat. I'm not at all presentable."

"It doesn't matter," said La Señorita, as ever elegant in black, as she settled herself on the leather banquette.

Estela could not tell if it did not matter where they were going, or that she did not have a hat. By now she knew that La Señorita had made up her mind about what was to happen that night, and that she, Estela, had no choice but to be swept along in her wake.

As the train pulled away from the station, the moon shone like hard, coconut candy in the sky, brittle and white, casting the buildings, as they passed, into sharp relief and shadow. The men in their white straw hats and trousers looked like paper cutouts in a Nativity scene. The houses became farther and farther apart, and the train picked up speed as they left the city. La Señorita was strangely quiet, the glowing tip of her cigarillo occasionally moving in the darkened train compartment. Estela must have dozed.

In what seemed like a moment, the train began to slow. Estela started awake to see La Señorita gathering her skirts around her. The conductor came to their car and stood by the door.

"Ready?" asked La Señorita. "We are going to disembark here."

"But the train hasn't stopped," said Estela, trying to peer into the night to see where they were.

"No matter," said La Señorita as the conductor opened the door.

As the train slowed, a small platform came into view, pale in the moonlight. With a firm grip, the conductor lifted first La Señorita, then Estela, out the open door into the capable hands of a strong youth. The train, which never did actually stop, picked up speed with a whistle and disappeared into the night.

La Señorita greeted the youth in the same familiar fashion as she had the conductor. He bowed and escorted them a few steps to a doorway, through which they stepped down into a room hot and bright with voices.

Estela looked about herself with astonishment. She was in a large, well-appointed room filled with tables. On each table stood a bottle of tequila or rum and a candle, and around each table was gathered a small group of women—talking, smoking, or playing cards. There was not one man in the room. The women were dressed in every manner imaginable, from traditional village dress to evening gowns to trousers, with pistolas on each hip, boots on the table. Estela could barely keep herself from staring. As La Señorita had assured Estela, it did not matter that she was not wearing a hat.

The women greeted La Señorita noisily, and she stepped forward into the crowd, waving and kissing and calling out names. A tall, striking woman stepped into the room from a doorway at the far end. She was dark and of exceptional beauty, dressed in a traditional white embroidered dress. She and La Señorita greeted each other with abrazos.

"This," said La Señorita to Estela, "is our hostess, the incomparable Doña Cata."

Estela greeted her shyly, but recognition was beginning to dawn. She was now in the famous mansion that Don Porfírio had built for his mistress, La Doña, one of the most powerful women in Mexico. She ruled her village like a man, and had acquired vast holdings of farmland and factories—much like La Señorita.

When they were seated at a table, Estela leaned forward and asked, "How can these women be out at this hour without their husbands?"

La Señorita threw back her head and laughed. Estela had never seen her like this.

"These women answer to no men," said La Señorita. "These are the mistresses of power. The men have their Congress, but the women have Doña Cata's." La Señorita looked around the room. "This is the only reason there are health checks for the working women on the streets," she said, "and any schools at all that accept female students. Don't think for a minute that the men would have thought of these things on their own, or approved of them. Still," she said, sighing, "there is so much left to do."

Estela tried to look around discreetly. Some of the faces looked familiar, but most of them were unknown to her. This did not surprise her, since many of these women were never seen in public, at least not officially. Estela tried to imagine which woman was with which prominent man in the government. La Señorita tried to help her out.

"That's Doña Reina, who goes with Senator Gonzalvo-Bilboa," she whispered, "and that's the proprietress of one of the most expensive houses in the District, Doña Carmela."

The men would take their wives, if any woman at all, to official functions, including those held by La Señorita to raise money for the school. Still, as La Señorita introduced Estela to them, a few said, "Oh, yes," as though they knew who she was, and some even said, "The Woman in Grey," as though it were her title. She wondered if, in their minds, she was associated with Victor Carranza.

Estela could hear conversations about banking and transportation, about the best colleges in Europe, the best sea routes to get there, and who had just acquired a prized painting for her collection. The finest, hand-rolled cigarettes were offered to each table, the best rum and tequila and even sherry. Someone in a corner strummed a guitar that was almost impossible to hear beneath the shrill and hearty voices. As the noise and laughter swirled around them, Estela managed to choke down a glass of sherry. She was also served cool water, a commodity more precious in the Capital, right now, than liquor.

The voices seemed to grow louder as time passed, until Estela could not tell one from the other. She nodded and smiled dumbly when she thought she had been addressed, but really, Estela could not understand a thing. All around her, the women laughed and talked familiarly, calling one another "cara" and "maja"—dear and queen. In a farther corner, two of them embraced and kissed in a rather intimate manner, oblivious, it seemed, to the crowd around them. Estela was beginning to understand what La Señorita meant by the phrase, "women who answer to no men."

After about an hour, as far as Estela could tell, the guitarist put down her instrument and clapped her hands sharply several times. The room stilled, and the claps were answered by claps from the doorway in the same, staccato pattern. The guitarist continued to clap in rhythm as several women in embroidered huipiles over white skirts entered the room, stepping and stopping in unison. When they reached the center of the room, the four of them stood facing one another, two facing two in a square, and began a dance accompanied only by the percussive clapping of hands and the surprisingly forceful stomping of bare feet. Their faces were serious, their eyes shining.

Soon others joined them from the tables, in all manner of dress, until there were two lines of eight facing each other. The sound and motion, repeated over and over, yet too complex a pattern to remember the first time heard and watched, was intoxicating.

At some point they stopped, and one of the women sang a mournful song in a language Estela did not recognize. The original four exited the way they had come, stepping and stopping, stepping and stopping, while the others returned to their seats.

La Señorita had disappeared at some point during this dance, and Estela looked about the room to see where she might be. Then she heard that laugh again, the one La Señorita had uttered upon their arrival, and Estela saw her coming in the door arm in arm with La Cata. La Cata was smiling and shaking her head no, no, as several women entreated her, then seemed to relent with a shrug and a smile as a chair was pulled out for her at a table.

La Doña Cata was said, by some, to be a sorceress, a diviner. Bottles and glasses were cleared away from the table, and she spread a deck of playing cards. As she turned them face up, one by one, the other women, now standing and gathered around, murmured and exclaimed.

The sixth card La Cata turned up was the King of Diamonds. The seventh was the Jack of Hearts. As Estela craned her neck to see, there was something about the Jack that looked different to her. She couldn't quite place her finger on it. Something about the length of the hair or the curl of the lip that made the figure look both masculine and feminine.

La Cata surveyed the cards and took a long draw on her cigarette. "The drought will end," she said, placing her hands flat on the table over the cards, "when the fathers acknowledge their daughters."

This was met by cheers and gritos, and La Cata swept up the cards into a compact bundle and left the room.

"But what does she mean?" murmured Estela. "How can she know that?" No one answered her.

When La Señorita could see that Estela was about to wilt, she stood up, and along with several other women, took leave of the assembly. At the door, La Señorita brushed Doña Cata's lips with a cool kiss, and Estela felt an ugly thrill in her stomach, as though she could not tell if she had wanted to see that or not. They stepped out into the cool night air as a train light became visible in the distance. With the same agility with which they had disembarked, the women boarded the train north and took their seats in the otherwise empty car. In Mexico City, the familiar carriage was there to greet them, and Estela fell into it and did not remember getting into her bed before hearing the cock crow. All she noted was the thin mustache of cloud that passed before the face of the moon.

✳

Elsewhere, deep in the night, after the priests had gone to bed, the Virgin of Guadalupe left alone with her candles and her baby Jesus, young girls came out to dance. They were dressed in white chemises—stitched by their mothers of purest cotton—and they danced under the clear night sky to bring down the clouds, to bring down the old men on horseback to kiss the young girls and graze the earth with their cloudy horses. As the drought had deepened, more and more girls came out each night—arms and heads bare, bodies visible beneath the white gossamer dresses—and danced for the sky. Ancient songs went up, songs that hadn't been heard out loud for a long time, rising up into the dry darkness to entreat the old chaacs to come down and visit the daughters of the bat-faced Coyolxauhqui. Children of the moon, the girls danced and danced, first in random motions, then in faster, circular motions, raising their arms in an ecstasy of trance and sleep deprivation. For every morning in the quiet before dawn, these same girls put on their skirts and huipiles and rebozos and carried what potable water remained to their masters and mistresses, ground the corn, kneaded the masa, and cooked the tortillas for a million souls.

Floors went unscrubbed, however, and the streets unwashed, so that the reek of the city changed from its odiferous, tropical smell to the ripeness and stench of death. Dogs and horses were dropping in the streets. Wails of mourning rose from the barrios, the roadside, the dirt lane, as babies died of diarrhea from the contaminated liquids fed to them, or from no liquids at all.

✳

In the secret convents, the nuns were praying. Don Porfírio, indirectly of course, through his young second wife, asked that there be no raids on their illegal convents by the civil police during this time, so that they might pray for rain uninterrupted. In a certain part of the Capital, not too far from Chapultépec Park, old men were bowing and praying. Was this a sign? Had the corrupt government of Porfírio Díaz, built on the backs of the poor, been struck by plagues like Pharoah's army?

The earth had become so dry that the snakes had crawled out of their holes in disgust. There were grinding, cracking noises from deep beneath the ancient buildings as the normally damp soil contracted and compacted under their weight.

And the young girls danced, round and round, faces turned up, tempting the old water gods to come down, come down, and taste the curve of their young lips, caress the taut flesh of their young bodies, and leave their horses in the thirsty fields to graze.

BETO

Only one man was allowed to pass beyond the gates of La Paciencia, and he had no legs.

As Lent drew to its mournful conclusion, one evening Estela left the school a little later than usual. Since carriages were banned until Holy Saturday, most of the wealthy had departed Mexico City for the duration. Estela was walking to el Paseo de Bucareli, which was not far, at least in distance.

She heard a hissing noise from the shadows. "Ese," it said, and a man stepped out, looking her up and down. "La Palomita, I remember you."

Estela ignored him and walked on.

"Palomita," he called, hurrying after. "Don't you remember me? I left you a very nice present."

When he grabbed her arm, Estela swung around long enough to see the bloodshot eyes, too close to hers, and catch a whiff of his vile, inebriated breath. Her parasol struck the side of his head with the force of her turn, sending him to the ground, where he screamed epithets after her hurrying figure.

Poor Palomita, she thought, the next time he visits the real one.

The rains had come early, after the months of pestilential drought, and the ground was saturated and heaving. It seemed to breathe and suppurate, the loose stones and bricks shifting in the mud that covered everything. Some streets were completely impassable, the water risen above the walkways and entering the ground floors of the buildings along them. All manner of vile things floated in this muck, and Estela, still shaken by her encounter with La Palomita's suitor, picked her way gingerly through it.

From this miasma rose a sound, almost like a moan, as Estela made her way down one street. "Señora," it seemed to say, and she shuddered when she heard it again, a harsh, insistent voice. "Señora!"

Stopping, she stared at a particularly repulsive-looking mass, and it spoke again. "Por favor, señora, help me," the earth seemed to say.

Fighting her impulse to hurry on, Estela took hold of a protrusion with both hands and, bracing her feet, pulled. She pulled and pulled until first one limb and then another was loosened from the tarlike substance that the streets had become. When it was freed from the mud and filth that had held it plastered to the ground, it sat up, and Estela discovered that, in its own grotesque way, it was a man. For a fleeting moment of despair, she thought that it might even be her husband, Zacarías, for beneath the grime, this man had the same look of another world in his eyes. But she realized, upon righting the figure, that he was too stocky, too broad in the shoulders. In addition, he had no legs.

Since she was not too far from the school, which she had left moments before, Estela returned and enlisted the help of Rosalinda. Rosalinda hoisted the man across her back, unmindful of the filth and grime that stained her habits, and carried him back to the courtyard. They wrapped him in a blanket and placed him by the outdoor stove to the back of the courtyard, near the corral. Free of the muddy street and filled with hot food, the man soon revived enough to tell his tale. The women gathered around and listened.

"Call me Beto," he began.

Far to the north, where the desert sang his true name, the man had been born in an Opata village. He was the youngest of five and from an early age had been able to predict the future and interpret dreams. He could also predict the past, and knew things about his homeland that even the elders had forgotten.

"There is a valley where we lived," he said in a harsh whisper that caused his listeners to lean forward, "and it was very beautiful. It was rich and green and full of game. There was a river that gave us all that we needed, as long as we were thankful and observed the fiestas and holy days. We had cattle and horses, and grew wheat, as people do in the north. There were wild birds and fruits, and the annual Fiesta de Magdalena."

The women sighed, remembering their village fiestas.

"But things changed," he said, his tone becoming bitter. "The people turned away from God. The vecinos came and stole our land, and the Apaches came and stole our livestock. There was much killing. We were starving."

The women began to provide a chorus of affirmation, a response to the call of his story.

"I just know a little of these things, because I was very young, thank God, and spared the worst. My mother took me away to a place called Casas Grandes, where she heard that there was a great healer who had come to unite the Indian people."

At this, Estela, who had begun to drift away on the current of his words, focused on the face of the man. She could barely make it out in the dim light, except for his intense eyes. On inspection, Beto seemed very young, hardly older than her own son, but his demeanor was that of an aged man.

"But the authorities came, soldiers came, and there was much killing. My mother and her husband were killed, but I was saved. They say that just before she died, my mother passed me through a hole in a wall, to people who escaped. I was raised by another family along with their own children."

"And the healer?" asked Estela in a weak voice. "What was he called?"

"They called him El Tecolote, the voice of the owl. My people tried to get rid of their enemies by sending them owls to speak to them and curse their dreams. I'm not sure if this man was sent to curse us or the authorities, but in the end, it is all the same—the poor suffer."

At this there was a murmur of assent from all the listeners. Estela felt herself growing a little faint by the flickering light of the fire, and sat down on a stone bench nearby.

"You are from the north," said Hermelinda. "Did you hear of these things?"

"Yes," said Estela. "They happened all the time."

The women sighed and wiped their eyes, and Beto began to weave one tale after another of his travels and tribulations. As a young man, he had worked as a scout, helping the United States Army to route the Apaches along the Arizona border. He had picked fruit and built churches. He had been everywhere, riding the ferrocarril as it was extended across the country, even far into el norte, the northern territories that were now occupied by the Norte Americanos, as far west as California and Oregon, as far east as places that the women did not recognize.

"And your legs?" asked one. "What happened to your legs?"

"Ah, my legs," said Beto, patting his thigh. "I have lived without them so long, I forgot I started out with them."

And he told the story of a train ride, and the spells that he suffered, indeed had probably been suffering when Estela found him, that took him from this world and let him see things from near and far. But he could not guard his body during those times, and so it was susceptible to danger. He had fallen beneath the iron wheels of a train on which he had been riding. A young doctor had saved him, keeping him from bleeding to death by applying a hot iron to the stumps of his legs, but doomed him to life as a cripple. Estela noticed his hands, how the backs of his knuckles had turned into huge, callused surfaces, like hooves. His skin was crisscrossed with thousands of scars, like a road map of sorrow.

"And so you see me," said Beto, "half a man, but the right half."

"And what did you see this time?" asked another.

Beto looked straight at Estela, who sat dreaming in the twilight, looking sad.

"I saw a house of stone. A house full of beautiful women who would take me in."

At that, the women laughed and teased him, telling him that no man had ever lived at La Escuela de la Paciencia.

"In fact," said Corona, unusually bold, "the boys must leave when they turn twelve. They must go and find work."

"Ah, I won't stay," said Beto. "I have work to do, too. Many people need my help. You see," he said, holding up his arm, "my mother tied this around my wrist when I was small, to keep the bad spirits away, so I can venture into the dreams of others without getting hurt."

The women marveled at the grimy red string that was knotted in an elaborate bracelet around his wrist. For Beto was one of those men who live between sleeping and waking, between this life and the next, and are granted visions that most of us are too fainthearted to endure. Estela doubted that the string talisman had been there that long, dirty as it was, but she had heard of such things. The memories these events brought back had begun to make her heart ache, and she noticed that the man continued to stare at her. She wondered how much he could read in her heart.

After a while, Chepa, a woman who seldom spoke at all, began to tell of her childhood, and Estela learned things about her that she had never suspected before. It turned out that she had come from a village on the Rio Yaqui and shared many of Beto's memories of the land and a sacred attachment to it. The seven holy villages of the Yaqui, she said, were where Jesus had walked. The Yaqui had tried again and again to regain dominion over their homeland, even encouraging the French occupation in return for a promise of sovereignty. What did they care if the French or the Spanish controlled Mexico City, as long as the indigenous people of the north could be free?

Like Beto's father, the Yaqui men were taken from their families and shipped off to work as slaves in unhealthy climates, the authorities probably hoping that they would die of disease and loneliness. Many did. Others were slaughtered and dumped in the bay of Guaymas. Estela had never heard of these things, but each atrocity that Chepa recounted was echoed, in some form, by another woman. Chepa herself had escaped from a plantation in the Yucatán and come to Mexico City with a soldier who had befriended her.

One after another of the women chimed in, like a chorus of crickets at night, with memories of their girlhoods in small towns and villages, far from the noise and rumble of la Ciudad. The dim light of the fire provided a soft cover under which they could speak truths, their expressions hidden in the folds of their rebozos. Almost all of them, Estela learned, had come to the city held by the scruff of the neck in the teeth of starvation.

Estela felt an odd thrill pass through her as she heard these stories. It was as though she had known about them, but not known them. It was a hidden history of her country, as though a stone had been turned over to reveal the life underneath. She felt as though she were staring into an inky dark well, images rising to the surface and accusing her—of what she was not sure, but it had something to do with her life of relative ease and privilege. Although she had suffered, she had not suffered like these women.

The villages were dying, she realized, as the land was taken away from the people, and the monstrous size of Mexico City grew and grew. Each hacienda, with a single owner, replaced communal land that had supported many villages. Each railroad line cut through land that had been cultivated since the beginning of the world.

Now the villagers cut cane and processed it into rum for the wealthy landowners to export, and bought their food from a company store—always in debt, always behind. They were paid in wormy cornmeal and soap that had the company name on it. They raised food that they were not allowed to eat, mined precious metals to be taken by someone else, forged iron parts for the voracious factories that were consuming the countryside.

When a man died or was injured, his family was left without a house or resources. They wrapped up their bundles and moved to the City, where—they had heard—they could be paid in real money for their labors, beholden to no one. The boys worked as day laborers, and the girls worked as maids or cooks or laundresses until they got too old or too ugly, or pregnant by the husband or his sons. Then it was back to the streets. This was La Señorita's story again, but told by the women themselves.

Estela returned late to her quarters at La Señorita's house. Besides her muddy clothes and disheveled hair, Estela had a wild look in her eye.

La Señorita sat in the half-light by the fire, ruminating on who knew what mystery. "What kept you out?" asked La Señorita, who seldom kept track of Estela's comings and goings.

"We found a man in the street, a man with no legs, and we took him in and fed him."

This told La Señorita what had happened, but not why Estela seemed so affected by it. "And?"

"And he told stories, and we all sat and listened. He is from the north, from where"—Estela hesitated—"people I used to know once lived. It was very sad," she added.

La Señorita sat and watched Estela as she gazed into the fire, and neither could guess what was in the heart of the other.

✶

The man called Beto dozed in the courtyard that evening but was gone by first light.

He returned every few weeks, each time appearing suddenly, silently at twilight in front of the gate. Estela had instructed the keeper to always let him in. Beto was inevitably surrounded by the women, who brought him choice food and treated him as the son from whom they had long been lost. Because he was eye level with them, children showed him their projects and school lessons. They told him things they would tell no other adult, knowing he could keep a secret.

The women usually took the shirt from his muscular back and replaced it with a clean one, washing and mending the soiled one, or brought him a new blanket. Each little tear in one of his shirts was lovingly repaired with embroidery based on one of his stories, so that after a time, his shirts were a riot of story and memory. They became covered with flowers and birds, stone houses and thatched roofs, corn in all its forms, lovers and rivals, caciques and farmers, maids and matriarchs, trees, rivers, and song.

Even without legs, moving about by the propulsion of his strong arms in a crude, hopping motion, Beto seemed to have roots that extended far beneath the surface of the earth, and tied him to the memories that we all share. Estela suspected that he visited other communities throughout the city, perhaps in the countryside as well, replenishing his cache of stories. He paid for his time in the courtyard with accounts of his latest adventures, by interpreting dreams and making predictions, and by calling back the precious memories of the dead, of whom we all know so many, and whom we will join all too soon.

hile Isabela and Graciela taught evenings at La Paciencia, they continued to live at home with their father, to whom they were greatly attached. As a precaution, Estela sent Noé home with them on the evenings they taught, since it was not too far away, and he was now a capable young man. Estela was concerned that they not get distracted on the way and fall into their old habits. Noé seemed to enjoy these evenings and evinced a new interest in learning and philosophy.

All of this was well and good until the day that Señor Pelegrino came to the school to call on Estela. Corona came to the corner room where Estela maintained a little desk, trying to sort out the business affairs of La Paciencia. In the back of her head was a jumbled ball of thoughts concerning her own affairs, but as usual, she ignored these in favor of the more solvable.

"Directora," said Corona at the door, "Señor Pelegrino is here to see you."

"Yes?" said Estela. "Then show him in."

"He seems . . . unhappy," said Corona enigmatically, and drifted away.

Pelegrino came in clutching his hat with great agitation. Estela invited him to sit, but he did so only after glancing about the room with great disdain, as though the very premises would contaminate him.

"I have come to tell you that your son has further corrupted my daughters," he said bluntly.

"What? My son? What are you talking about?"

Pelegrino went on to describe the scene upon which he had happened the previous evening. It had so upset him that he had dismissed his classes early in order to come see Estela. His daughters, who had not come to the school that day, were confined at home.

It had begun innocently enough, Estela later learned from Noé. He was deeply ashamed to recount these events to his mother. Isabela and Graciela had, indeed, begun to share their vast knowledge of philosophical inquiry with Noé on their short walks back to the pensión. The discussion on the previous evening had turned to the meaning of matter—of substance and insubstance, and eventually to whether we exist or merely imagine that we exist.

"I argued," said Noé, "according to what I have learned at school, that it would be illogical to imagine that we exist if we did not. And with what would we imagine this? One needs to exist in order to imagine anything. I recounted Aristotle's classifications of reality—substance, quantity, quality, relation, action, passion, position, condition, and the determination of time and place.

"Isabela and Graciela, however, argued that we have no way of knowing whether or not we exist. We can only substantiate our beliefs through our senses. And if we, in fact, exist only in the imagination of another, say, as in a dream, how can we then verify our existence? They called this concept *maya,* and said that it originated with the Hindus—the concept that we may exist wholly as a dream.

"But *I* said that cannot be possible, because we are able to *control* our behavior," Noé went on, now quite caught up in re-creating the discussion. "And because we can feel sensation at will. This is not possible in a dream. I then pinched myself to show that I could cause myself pain."

"'But sensation,' said Graciela, 'is at the mercy of emotion. And where, in our corporeal being, does emotion reside?'

"'How so?' I asked. 'Descartes said, "I think, therefore I am." Did he mean that he was dreaming? No, he meant that he existed.' By now, we had arrived at their rooms, and their father was out. I simply went inside to continue the discussion. I could not leave it incomplete, could I?"

Estela remained mum.

"At this point Isabela removed the upper part of her dress and took my hand and placed it on her . . . her body," said Noé, mumbling now. "It all happened so quickly, and I became confused. And she said, 'Can you tell now if Graciela is touching your back in one place or two?' And that is when Don Pelegrino came in. I could see that he was furious. He threw me out on the street. 'But sir!' I called out to him when I had regained my senses. 'We were merely discussing Descartes!'"

Even before hearing Noé's account of the events of that evening, Estela agreed with Señor Pelegrino that her son should no longer escort the young ladies home. Perhaps, she suggested, Pelegrino should come to La Paciencia and escort his daughters home himself, thus assuring their safety.

"And you, señora, need to teach manners to your son," said Pelegrino, rising to go, "as well as respect for the honor of women."

Estela sighed her assent. "But you know, we cannot supervise them forever."

"I hope that the Lord sends understanding husbands for my daughters," said Pelegrino. "Soon."

"With or without husbands," said Estela, "I suspect that your daughters will have a singular destiny."

"Forgive me, señora," he said, breaking, for the first time that day, his wall of indignation. He looked abashed. "I meant no offense to you personally."

"None taken," said Estela, smiling slightly. "But don't take your daughters from us. They have done a great deal of good, and I think that it has been good for them as well. We live in a new time, Señor Pelegrino, and perhaps there will come a day in which what we do will be as important as what people say about us."

✳

Estela was less clear about what was good for Noé. For once, she missed her long-departed husband, for despite his frequent absences, she did not recall any similar incidences with her eldest, Gabriel.

"Perhaps they occurred, but you never knew about them," suggested La Señorita. "All boys have such moments. It sounds to me as though your son has found the happy conjunction of the Temple of Minerva and the Temple of Venus, of learning and sensual delight. What better introduction to the great mysteries of life? In some families, the fathers assure that their sons are initiated into the mysteries of carnality with the help of a professional. And believe me, they do not discuss Descartes."

Estela shuddered at the thought. "Perhaps this wasn't so bad. But who knows where it might have led if Pelegrino had not returned just then?"

La Señorita smiled. "He is becoming a man, Estela. Some families are headed by boys as young as your son. Remember, the eldest male in a family is legally responsible for them. In fact, as your oldest male relative on the premises, your son is legally responsible for you."

"Don't tell him," said Estela.

"He will discover this soon enough."

✳

Estela decided that Noé could be kept busy by helping out even more with her work at La Paciencia. The printer M Cardoz had known Noé since he was a young boy, because Noé sometimes accompanied his mother to his ethereal premises. Cardoz agreed that Noé could bring materials for *La Linterna,* and he became the messenger to the mysterious printer who moved his shop as fate and the winds of change dictated. Noé continued to visit his grandparents, even without his mother. She was more and more preoccupied with her work, with her mysterious disappearances that had something to do with *La Linterna,* but perhaps had more to do with Victor Carranza.

At the lyceo, Noé was taught the prevailing philosophy and arts of the time. His schoolmasters were proud to be part of the Porfírian era, of the optimistic mood of progress and scientific dispassion that could be applied to the ills of society. According to their way of thinking, in order to stave off cold, people should bathe each morning in cold water. Thus, the circulatory system became immune to the effects of cold weather and would not require extra protection. Likewise, mothers should raise their children with logic and dispassion so that the young can see that it is a logical world, where consequences follow actions.

What Noé saw, however, were the sons of the wealthy enjoying the fruits of their fathers' business dealings. Because Noé lacked any family connections with whom his classmates were familiar, having originated in the provinces, he was generally excluded from their social activities. The schoolmaster told his students, with much smirking and derision, that when peasants near Mexico were recently introduced to modern plows with two handles, rather than one, they cut off the extra handle with a machete. Somehow this backwardness was associated with all people who originated outside of the city of Mexico, with the exception, perhaps, of one or two families from Puebla.

Noé discovered that his mother's work carried with it a
certain notoriety. From the time he was little, the women of the
streets had come up to him, petting him and cooing over him
as "el hijo de la Señora en Gris"—the child of the Woman in
Grey. His mother smiled tolerantly, if nervously. After all, if she
did not treat these women with respect, how could she expect
others to? The fact that his mother, like many of the street
women, had no husband to show for herself was not lost on
Noé. At times, Noé was derided for his mother's affiliation
with La Paciencia, but the connection with La Señorita Mejora
de Gonga, whose influence struck awe and caution in even the
crudest of schoolboys, kept this from getting out of hand. In
any case, he could not have afforded the trappings needed to
participate in polo or one of the other sports that were becoming popular among the elite of the capital.

✳

His best friend was a young intellectual, Samuel Gonsález
Trebiño, whose father lectured on the sciences. Like Noé, his
last name was of dubious origin, or at least its spelling was, but
his family had lived in Mexico City for several generations.
They knew of Noé's grandparents, Julio and Mariana, and
welcomed him into their home. Here, Noé found customs
and family ways that were familiar to him, and a blending of
philosophies that did not pit the secular against the spiritual
but presented them as two sides of the same whole.

Dr. Gonsález de Castro, while a respected mathematician
and student of the astral sciences, with a special interest in
discovering the lost knowledge of the Mayas, had no lack of
sentimentality for his five children. Dr. Gonsález delighted
in their accomplishments and participated in impromptu concerts with them, playing the violin along with their respective
instruments. Samuel's mother, while quiet and retiring, showed

a devotion to her husband and children that Noé found astounding, having witnessed so many women whose lives had been devastated by their relationships to their husbands. Saturday afternoons in their home, all work set aside, were devoted to the common pursuits of the family, and the harmony evident was a revelation to Noé.

Over the years, as Noé became privy to the emotional shadings of adult life, he gathered that his own father had abandoned his mother, whether for a spiritual quest or for more mundane reasons, he could not be sure. In public, he stuck with his mother's story that his father had been killed at Casas Grandes. But the fact that his grandparents spoke of Zacarías Carabajál as though he were still alive gave him hope as well. What did he hope for, Noé sometimes asked himself, a meeting? A reconciliation? An acknowledgment? Over and over in his mind, Noé had an image of climbing up the side of a mountain, following a streambed, to find a man standing knee-deep in the cold, rushing waters. Calling out to him, and having the man look up. He recognizes the man but cannot quite make out his features where they are shaded by his broad-brimmed hat from the harsh sunlight.

Noé imagined his father as existing on the edge of time, in that fleeting moment between the past and the future, that place that we all yearn for yet can never quite grasp. He knew that this was an idealization, one based in part on the light in his grandmother's eyes, but one that he could not dislodge from his mind.

In a time and place where the father was everything, from El Presidente on down, he hoped, perhaps, for a place in the greater order of things. For this was what was emphasized at school: order. Those who stepped out of line, either by entertaining ideas that were not directly in keeping with the Porfírian regime or by crossing the tangled lines of social status, were reviled and derided—the Indian with pretensions above his station as much as the well-born debaucher who fell to drinking in public in the wrong company. The papers were filled with cautionary tales about such people.

At the same time, Noé sensed that his mother had been, from the beginning, complacent with this situation. His grandparents did not seem to blame either of them for the separation but praised them both warmly when given the opportunity. At least his nona did. Watching her work in her garden, turning the earth with a small, spoonlike implement, rescuing herbs from the heat of the day and adding them to her cooking pot, Noé found a solace that he felt nowhere else. And in the grace of her hands, their cool, dry touch cupping his face, he found an affirmation of life.

His grandfather, in spite of being steeped in so much knowledge accumulated over time, would not discuss the past. Seldom outdoors anymore, unless led by Mariana, Julio was more and more concerned with what he called the future. With him, Noé was able to discuss the ideas that were put forth in his classes and among his classmates. Noé sometimes read him the papers and described to him the changes that were going on all around them.

"Look below the surface," Don Julio would say. "Below the first layer is another, and another."

Dr. Gonsález agreed. "People are often satisfied with first impressions," he said, "even the educated, who should know better. An American started a farm near the city a couple of years ago," he went on, "and used a steel plow to turn the soil much more quickly and efficiently than is possible with the old wooden plows. His corn came up tall and lush, taller than a man's head. But at the end of the season, a windstorm came through the region. His corn was toppled, and the crop ruined. But the corn of his Indian neighbors, short and held in place by the hard soil, showed no damage at all. After that, the American sold his plow and allowed the old methods to continue in use on his land."

Noé told the story about the plow handle, as told to him in school, to his grandfather. "Change has not always been good for los de abajo," he responded. "First came the Aztecs, then the Spaniards, and now all of these other foreigners who would rip the heart out of this country and carry it home like a trophy. In every case, progress has been of cost to the Indians, whose land is inevitably confiscated in order to be put to better use. What better use than for a man to feed his family?"

Noé also confided to his grandfather how their origins in the north were seen as a sign of his backwardness and provincialism.

Julio pondered this idea for a moment. "Change is like a disease," he responded. "Those of us in el norte, by being exposed to los vecinos, the neighbors to the north for so long, have gradually gotten used to it, and don't get all feverish when we encounter something new. In the Capital, on the other hand, a new idea sweeps through the city like cholera. One person gets a bicycle, everyone needs a bicycle."

"It's true," agreed Dr. Gonsález when Noé recounted what his grandfather had said. "Many of the families here feel that ideas from abroad, especially, must be better than ideas from here. That's why everything that happens in Paris is mimicked here. Many of these people do not feel secure in their own backgrounds, feel inferior, and so try to make themselves better through imitation. Unfortunately, bad taste often governs what ideas are adopted. There is no judgment as to what is appropriate for our people, or even aesthetically pleasing."

At the Gonsález house, Noé learned about music, literature, and the vast body of sciences. When he described the capacious library to his grandfather, with its volumes on Galileo,

Euclid, Archimedes, Copernican theory, Newton, and Johannes Kepler, Noé realized, too late, that he had evoked a great nostalgia in the elderly man for his own lost tomes.

"In my head," said Don Julio, "I have a great library." And he went on to quote passages from several books of the Cabala, from Corrado Guidetti, Isaac Gershon, Moses Maimonedes, and Isaac Orobio de Castro—books published in Spain, Italy, the Netherlands, and Portugal over hundreds of years of time. Noé learned that the old man had once had access to translations of the Bible, classical rabbinical literature, and the major philosophic works of the Middle Ages. He had once handled the *Vindiciae Judaeorum,* the apologia of Yshac Cardoso called *Las excelencias y calunias de los Hebreos,* treatises on the 613 commandments, halakhic manuals, and abridgments of the *Shulhan'Arukh.* Don Julio even claimed to have had a sample of the secret writings of Francisco Maldonado da Silva, written in charcoal ink with a pen made from the bone of a chicken, on scraps of paper joined together, produced in his prison cell in Lima under the name Eli Nazareno. All burnt to a crisp. And with it, Noé realized, any chance that he himself might ever have more than a passing acquaintance with this body of knowledge.

"'Their investigations are divine,'" quoted Don Julio from Cardoso, "'and divine their conclusions, compared to which, human subtleties are spiderwebs of little substance.'"

Since Noé's unfortunate, if blissful, encounter with Graciela and Isabela, which had turned their father against him, Estela had deemed it necessary to keep him otherwise occupied. In addition to his studies at the lyceo, she had enlisted his help in writing for both *Viajes* and *La Linterna* under various pseudonyms. Although not even an adolescent when he started, he had been coached in the language of the ladies of the Capital to describe costumes and social events, and to provide domestic advice in *Viajes*. For *La Linterna*, he did not actually write the articles, which generally had to do with things far beyond his experience or ken, but was, at times, asked to proof the pages with his mother or Gloria Quinque.

Thus, from an early age, both in the doings of La Paciencia and his own encounters with the greater world, Noé learned that there were two worlds—los de abajo y los de arriba—and that he had a place in neither. Or a place in both, depending on how he looked at it. This gave him a somewhat detached air that made him appear to be unapproachable to some. When greeted with warmth, however, he responded in kind. Noé became known at school for his ability to debate all sides of an issue. He could convince an opponent, without reservation, of the absolute correctness of his viewpoint—causing the fellow not only to agree but apologize profoundly for ever thinking otherwise—then turn around and argue the opposing premise with the same fervor with which he had defended the first. The sight of him standing and waving his narrow hands in the face of a would-be gladiator in the arena of ideas became a sought-out pastime for the young men of the city who were not occupied with more physical pursuits.

Noé did well in his studies, and La Señorita encouraged him to pursue course work at the university level. La Señorita, with no children of her own, or even family that Estela could discern—although she sometimes referred to elderly relatives who lived in the countryside—took a particular interest in Noé's progress.

"Why don't you study law?" she suggested. "You certainly have the demeanor for it. That would be good preparation for going into politics, although you don't really have the family connections for a public life."

"Please don't," said Estela suddenly. "Isn't there enough trouble in the world?"

Noé was surprised at his mother, who seldom expressed an opinion on anything outside of her particular environment. In spite of La Señorita's suggestion, he took his mother's concerns to heart and enrolled at the university to study language and philosophy. Estela, who never complained about the cost of his education, continued to pay his tuition.

One morning as he prepared to go to his classes, Noé saw his mother slip something furtively into her purse. Had she not done so in such a secretive manner, he was sure he never would have noticed the gesture. Shortly after, she prepared to go out. Noé went downstairs, but instead of leaving for the university, he stepped into a small alcove and waited until his mother left. Then he followed her at a distance.

She walked. Up the beautiful Paseo de Bucareli, then to the right along the edge of the Alameda, where the gardeners were grooming the lush grounds that were reserved for people of the better classes. Down along the walkways, past the shops filled with wonderful, imported goods. At a shop window, she paused to look inside, then continued walking. Upon passing the window himself, Noé saw that she was looking at a brightly hued dress, lavender with pale yellow insets.

On she strolled, oblivious to the street vendors shouting as she passed, the carriage drivers who would trample the unwary pedestrian, the small churches that competed with the cathedral, note for note, with their own constantly pealing bells. Estela paused only once, to hand a coin to a beggar woman, before entering a cavernous building across from the Zócalo.

Noé was amazed to see that it was the Monte de Piedad. His mother walked down the crowded aisles as though this were a second home, nodding to certain people as she passed, never losing her regal bearing or her placid air. She walked to a counter at the back, where a clerk in wire-rim spectacles greeted her by name, and with a small bow. Then, as Noé watched, she pulled a velvet bag from her purse and placed it on the counter. The clerk looked briefly inside, then produced paperwork for Estela to sign. He then counted out a number of bills and Estela placed them in her modest purse. The whole encounter took less than five minutes. Estela then left by a far entrance and returned to La Señorita's manorial home on the good side of Bucareli.

All of that day as he attended his classes, Noé was consumed by curiosity about his mother's transaction. He was so distracted that he nearly let a fellow student win a debate over the merits of allowing foreigners to own property in Mexico. All of that evening as well, Noé continued to wonder about the velvet bag and its contents. He had just caught a glimpse of something shining, a scatter of light reflected off of a faceted surface. Noé wondered if his mother was in financial trouble, or if this was something she did at La Señorita's bidding. He had pretty much convinced himself of the latter by the beginning of the next month, when he bade good-bye to his mother for the day. It was the beginning of a new school term.

"Here," she said, as she had so often before, "is the money for your tuition."

Only then did Noé realize the significance of the velvet bag and why the clerk at Monte de Piedad knew her so well.

✱

After that day, Noé began to seek out paid work on his own. He wrote reviews and articles for the many newspapers, journals, advertisers, and broadsheets that proliferated in that time and place. Under cover of various noms de plume, he tried to vary his style as was appropriate for the venue and subject matter. It soon became a diversion in the city to see who could spot an article written by Noé.

La Señorita realized that she was in danger of losing access to his talent, and began to pay him for his columns in *Viajes,* where, in the guise of a monk, he provided fatherly advice to newlyweds. She warned Noé to keep a low profile, as he was beginning to draw the attention of the authorities through his other work. While many newspapers were published, few dared print the unvarnished truth, especially about Don Porfírio himself. It was to those papers that Noé was drawn, supplying them with graphic stories about the lives of the poor.

Once, upon handing M Cardoz an especially inflammatory issue of *La Linterna,* in which women were encouraged to protect themselves from the brutality of the men in their lives, an issue full of horrible stories and lurid illustrations, Noé had the temerity to ask the self-contained man how he was able to print such things, if they did not, in fact, bother him.

"What is it like to write such things?" asked the printer.

Noé tried to hide his surprise that Cardoz knew him as one of the writers of these articles. "To put words on paper is to become someone else," he said, and shrugged.

"And to print them is to multiply the effect, becoming everyone, or no one," the printer replied. "To publish is to express the public thoughts of the people, and fan their secret desires as well. We all wish success to the successful, but tempered with a little humility. We wish swift justice done to the unjust, blessings to the humble, joy to the sad. A broadsheet provides a verisimilicrum of these things, if not the actual event. By telling tales that end the way they ought to, rather than the way they probably did, we provide the helpless public with a huge sigh of relief.

"There, skewered on the page," he went on, "is the corrupt politician, the inept legislator, the complacent judge. There, for all to see, is the murderess caught red-handed, the drunken husband, the ungrateful son."

"But," said Noé, frowning, "no one person can speak for everyone."

"No," said Cardoz, "but we can express the things people are unable or unwilling to express for themselves, that the world should have order, but not necessarily the order of the authorities in power. We remind them that there is a higher order of truth, beauty, and honor, an order that is impervious to the whims of the rich."

"So we are a voice for the poor?" asked Noé.

"In a way," said Cardoz. "Under the circumstances, we must do God's work, for outside of the Church, we must represent, in words and pictures, the arrangement of the world between Heaven and Earth, the rich and the poor. And perhaps," he added, "a little below the earth as well, where the Prince of Darkness rules."

Was that a smile in his eyes? Noé could not be sure. It was, perhaps, the first time he had heard a joke from this otherwise somber and taciturn man. Noé left the printer, wherever he was that day, musing on the possibility that he, too, was performing God's work.

WHO HAS PROMISED US TOMORROW?

usabia, who never did anyone any harm, was killed by a carriage when one of her chickens ran out into the street.

"But how could that happen?" asked Estela, numb with shock.

"She cannot see, she could not see the carriage."

"Yes, but what was she doing outside?"

"The chicken ran out. Eusabia followed before anyone could stop her."

The women looked away guiltily. No one had ever warmed up to the strange woman who preferred the company of fowl, and they all felt responsible for her demise.

"Those drivers go too fast anyway," said Estela. "It's a wonder we haven't all been killed."

"Who has promised us tomorrow?" said Corona.

This struck Estela as a very old sentiment for such a young woman to say, but then she realized that Corona was over a decade older than when they had started the school. And so was she. The previous year, they had found Josefina dead in her bed, dressed as though for a long journey—even to her shoes—and clutching a bundle of food. They had buried her that way.

After Eusabia's death, the eggs never tasted the same, no matter how much chile was added to them. Children who had eaten them eagerly before now turned away at the taste.

"The chickens are unhappy," the women said to one another over meals. "They miss Eusabia."

La Paciencia felt oddly empty these days. Two months earlier, the women in L'Orchestre Tangier, now gainfully employed at El Tivolí, had announced that they were moving into their own quarters. They had found two adjacent rooms in a boardinghouse, with agreeable terms, and felt that they were ready to live on their own. With La Señorita's blessing, they had taken the musical instruments with them, and El Profesor Murillo, now married to Hermelinda, would continue to act as their director.

Rosalinda, too, had moved on. Having saved every penny she earned at the printing house, she was able to purchase her own, decrepit press, which she promptly refurbished. She now rented a tiny alcove near the Plaza de Santo Domingo, where she also slept. Gloria Quinque, who had wanted to publish a newsletter devoted exclusively to the formal education of women, was Rosalinda's first customer. She, along with her sisters in the Yucatán, were in the process of organizing a conference on women's rights.

"This was the point of the school, was it not?" said La Señorita. "To make these women independent?"

"Yes, of course," said Estela. "But I was attached to them. I enjoyed listening to them practice. It was a good influence on the others."

Although she would not say it to La Señorita, who seemed to possess no such frail attachments to others, Estela especially missed Hermelinda. The day that she returned with El Profesor, riding in a carriage like a fine lady, Estela had cried. Yes, she cried with happiness for her friend—who distributed sweets and kisses among the women in celebration of her nuptials, performed in Cuerna Vaca—but also with loss, for she knew that Hermelinda would no longer be a constant companion and source of practical advice. She would be too busy running her own household, and although Hermelinda promised to spend as much time as possible at La Paciencia, she was already making plans for her older children to join her.

The professor blushed and beamed, accepting the congratulations of the women, and clearly understood his good fortune. Estela could only pray that somehow she could manage without Hermelinda.

Although new women and children had immediately taken their places at La Paciencia, the atmosphere had changed. These women seemed younger and more desperate, with less of a sense of camaraderie. They looked at Estela with suspicion and distrust, unlike the earlier ones, who had treated her like a sister, or at least like a well-liked neighbor.

From outside the gates of La Paciencia, the news from everywhere was bad. Reports from the north, which seemed to originate in a far and alien country, spoke of uprisings and Apache invasions. Yet the official press continued to trumpet the glories of the Porfírian era, the triumph of order over chaos, of logic over superstition, of international economics over domestic self-sufficiency.

La Señorita waved away Estela's concerns. "You still have *Viajes* and *La Linterna*," she told her. With this, she implied Victor Carranza.

"I suppose so."

"Well, there is one thing I do not wish to see."

Estela could not imagine what La Señorita, in this world of sorrows, could possibly have not seen. "What might that be?"

"I do not wish to see the children of La Escuelita return with their own children, their own misfortunes. Bad enough they had to endure those of their mothers."

Estela's mind flew unbidden to the image of Rebeca's angelic hair and face, her white arm resting upon the desk, and shuddered. Where was she now? she wondered. Dead or borracha, her beauty long faded from this world.

✷

Estela had lived in La Señorita's house for many years now. The cook had long ago given up on keeping her from making her own coffee or washing out her own cup. Estela felt that she needed some domestic contact in order to feel as though she belonged somewhere.

La Señorita, on the other hand, felt no such compunctions. As far as Estela knew, La Señorita had never set foot in her own kitchen, leaving all such activities to her cook and housekeeper, even the arrangements for elaborate dinners. When she removed a wrap or hat, she always assumed that someone would be there to take it from her, not even glancing in their direction. She treated everyone—from her dressmaker to her solicitor—with equal weight, listening to what each had to say, then making decisions based on what she was told. She seemed to care about everything and nothing at once.

In spite of all the time Estela had known her, La Señorita was still a mystery. The night at La Cata's at the end of the drought had been the most revealing experience, but perhaps sensing Estela's discomfort, La Señorita had never taken her there again. The place existed in Estela's mind as a dream, or a nightmare, she wasn't sure which. But Estela understood that it fulfilled an important part of La Señorita's existence. She just didn't know how many other mysterious worlds La Señorita inhabited as well, compartmentalizing each so that one would not interfere with or impinge on the other.

Demeanor, as La Señorita had so often told Estela, was everything. Yet once or twice, Estela thought she had caught

La Señorita looking anxious, especially over financial matters. She wondered just how secure her financial empire was in the light of such radical change as seemed to be sweeping over the country.

✳

As for Victor Carranza, Estela felt that their relationship was that of an old married couple. If she broached any subject with him that he found objectionable, she would not hear from him for many weeks. At the same time, in no one else's company did she feel as free to be herself, to literally shed the grey dress and express her unfettered passions. She could tell that he felt the same way around her, could tell her things that La Señora de Carranza would neither understand nor condone. Their relationship was hemmed about with taboos and unspoken promises yet seemed a freer place than most of Mexican society. Perhaps that is why these relationships exist, thought Estela—by being forbidden, they were free.

While she herself seldom ventured out into society, Victor brought her his world, with all of the intrigues and scandals it contained. He told her of the doctors and lawyers, the famous orators and entertainers who visited the city from abroad. He repeated famous speeches in the legislature to her so that she might admire the sheer audacity of some of the speakers, and described the dinner parties of the rich to which he was invited.

Estela tried not to think about the domestic comforts provided by a wife and children, the quiet moments of companionship that she would never share. More than the public acknowledgment of her existence, these were what she missed the most. And these simple pleasures were what she had been denied in the first place by her own husband, Zacarías. Some things were never meant to be, she thought.

Then one day Victor Carranza came to their pensión in a state of agitation. "I have left my wife," he said, "and will sue for divorce."

"Why?" she asked.

"I have decided that we have lived this sham too long. It is time that we made things right between us." Victor paced up and down before the window, his mind racing as he talked.

"What are you talking about?" asked Estela. "I never asked you for this." She stood up from the chair where she had waited for him, the chair with the view of the tiny courtyard full of fruit trees.

"I know that you have not, and you have been very patient. But my children are old enough now to get by without my presence."

Estela knew that his youngest was only six; his oldest, the girl Noé had called La Princesa, barely fourteen.

"Did you have a fight?" she asked quietly. "Did she talk to you about me?" Estela tried to imagine this scene between them.

"It has nothing to do with her. I mean, it is just something that I have thought about for a long time."

"So what if you got a divorce? Then what? I have my work, I am a respectable woman in my own way."

"I know that we cannot marry under Mexican law if I am divorced, but we can go to the United States and marry. Would that suit you?"

Again, Estela could hardly believe what she was hearing. "Are you insane? What about Zacarías?"

Victor stopped. "What about Zacarías? Isn't he dead?"

"I have no way of knowing. I told you years ago that he was gone and would never return. And he has not."

"But you've told everyone that you are a widow."

Estela sat down again in exasperation. "I tell everyone that, but I don't know that for certain. I can't marry you in this country or in any country. And actually," she said, her temper rising, "I don't want to. What kind of a way is this to approach the subject? Didn't you think that I might have some opinion on this?"

Victor looked amazed. "You mean to say your husband could have come back at any moment? Just like that?"

"Yes," said Estela, snapping her fingers. "Just like that."

Now he looked angry. "Then you have deceived me."

"I never deceived you!" said Estela, standing again. "How dare you make such an accusation, you who stood in the street singing to me years ago, a respectable married woman, in front of all the neighbors!"

"Yes. But since you came to Mexico City, I thought that he was gone for good."

"He *is* gone for good," said Estela. "Just probably not dead. Or forgotten."

And with that, she realized it was true—he was not forgotten. Without a further word, she gathered her things and left.

Estela lay on her bed and stared at the ceiling. Noé came into the darkened room and found her, face wet with tears.

"Mamá," he said. "What is it? What has made you so sad?"

"Just life," she said. She had never spoken to her son about Victor.

"Are you crying over that doctor?"

She looked at him angrily. "And what if I am? What do you know about it?"

"Oh, Mamá," said Noé, sitting down on the side of the bed. "Don't you know that he isn't any good? I hear about his exploits from the other journalists."

"What exploits?" asked Estela suspiciously.

"Mamá," Noé looked around the room, looked at his hands. "He is a well-known man about town."

Estela sat up. "Go on."

Noé looked upset. "I thought you knew."

"Please tell me. I know nothing."

"Oh, he is like many of the men. He has had his fun. But recently he took up with a famous actress. They have been seen everywhere."

Estela felt a sensation of numbness creep up her hands, up her spine, until it clamped a chill hand upon her heart. "Well, since I don't go everywhere, I guess I haven't seen them."

"Please don't worry about him. He's not worth it. I'm sure whatever has existed between the two of you has not changed."

In spite of herself, Estela felt fresh tears springing from her eyes. "Oh yes it has," she said. "Oh yes it has."

"Besides," said Noé, patting her on the arm, "you have your work."

"Why does everyone keep saying that to me?" she said. "And how will we continue *La Linterna*?"

"Oh, leave that to me," said Noé. "I do most of it anyway. It doesn't have to be confined to those silly pictures. Let me handle it."

The weeks passed, and Estela went through the motions of living. Her heart felt frozen, immobile, as though it barely bothered to keep beating. She went to sleep each night imagining that she threw herself into the well of sorrows, eating the bitter dust at its bottom, filling her mouth with the broken shards of her life. She woke each day only to be overwhelmed with disappointment that she was still herself, that she was still alive. She dressed and went to La Paciencia, where she sat at her desk and stared at the papers. If Corona asked her to sign something, she did. At the end of the day, she could not remember what she had done, how she had even gotten from the house to the school and back again.

Eventually the freeze in Estela's heart was replaced with fire, with a deep and searing anger. She felt humiliated, duped. She wondered how she could be so oblivious to what everyone else knew, even her own son. She wondered how much the women at La Paciencia knew, if her private life was, in fact, a public drama, like those scandals in the broadsheets. People spoke gently to her, sensing her fragile mood, and she hurried in to close the door to her little office often, something she had seldom done before.

After much reflection, she decided that the argument with Victor had been staged. He had never intended to leave his wife for her, but rather, had wanted an excuse to leave Estela for his new mistress. She imagined him with the beautiful actress, making fun of Estela and her grey dresses, her conservative, old-fashioned ways from the provinces. She was well aware that actresses routinely bared their ankles and much more to God and all the world while onstage. Days passed when she could not eat a thing, when she could not bear the sight of a lady and a gentleman in a carriage together. She automatically averted her gaze lest she accidentally catch a glimpse of Victor and "esa mujer," as she came to call the actress to herself.

Estela suspected that he had deliberately pretended to misunderstand her marital status. She cringed at the thought that she had shared Victor with a variety of women. Bad enough to share him with a wife. She kept taking baths, washing and combing out her long hair. She cried in the bath, where no one, she thought, would notice her tears. Estela saw little of La Señorita during this time and did not know if she was deliberately avoiding her, or if she was simply caught up in her numerous projects.

*

Under Noé's direction, *La Linterna* grew more political.

"You need to be careful," said Estela, reviewing an issue in her office, "or the authorities will shut us down."

"Already," he said, smiling, "they send spies to follow me to the printer. But I've gotten used to eluding them. I jump over a wall and lead them into the teeth of a vicious dog, and they are usually gone for the day."

"And you know, you use too many words. If these women can't read, how can they understand what you are saying?"

"Someone will read it to them," he said. "I see it in the street every day. Every issue of *La Linterna* that we print is snatched up and read out loud in the courtyards and alleys of the poor. The aguajeros carry the information from house to house. Even some of the clergy, those who don't benefit from Don Porfírio, are using our ideas."

"That's lovely," said Estela, handing back the current issue. "Now you are writing sermons for priests."

Noé was pleased to detect a note of sarcasm in his mother's voice. It was the first time in weeks that he had seen her take an interest in anything. "You can tell women how to wash their babies all you want," he said, "but without land reform, there will be no future for the people of Mexico."

"Without live babies, there will be no people to work the land."

"All right," he said, bowing to her. "Every other issue will be on baby-washing."

"And nutrition," she said. "Don't forget about nutrition."

"Aye aye, mi capitán." Noé gave his mother a mock salute before ducking out through the doorway. It was the first time she had noticed how tall Noé had grown. Estela carefully folded the issue of *La Linterna* and placed it in the single drawer of her desk. She walked out into the courtyard and greeted the women who were winding up skeins of thread for embroidery. She could hear the children upstairs reciting their lessons, and her eye fell on a wooden trunk she had not noticed before. When Estela stooped to open it, she found that it was full of books.

"We have started a lending library for the women," said Isabela, walking up to stand beside her. "When someone is done, she returns it to the trunk for someone else to borrow. Since some of the women have learned to read, they want to keep in practice."

"But where did we get the books? These novels and adventures?"

"Well, Humberto brought some, and my sister and I gave a few insignificant things, and I think that La Señorita gave some poetry as well."

Estela smiled at her. Somewhere, she could hear Graciela giving a lesson in grammar. The smell of refried beans wafted across the courtyard, and Estela realized that she was hungry.

"Thank you," she said.

"It is nothing," replied Isabela. "It is we who should thank you. Sometimes I think that you do not realize all that you have done."

Estela looked down, unable to look her in the eye. "I think that I will have a little something to eat." She took a tortilla full of beans from the perpetually stirred pot in the corner of the courtyard and sat down in the sunshine on a stone bench, savoring the pleasure of humble food.

One day not long after, Victor Carranza's oldest daughter happened upon a strange man sitting in the walkway. She, along with her dueña, could not pass to the left or the right of him, there being a massive puddle of dubious content on the street side.

"Let us pass," said her dueña. "Can't you see that this is a young lady of quality?"

"And what qualities might those be?"

"Don't think I'm above giving you a good thrashing!" said the dueña, brandishing her parasol.

"Blessed Mother," he replied, "you wound me with your words. I am merely a poor beggar, seeking alms with which to keep body and soul together." He moved towards them with a curious hopping motion, propelling himself forward with his arms.

La Princesa could see that the man had no legs. Also, he wore a beautifully embroidered shirt, very fine in its detail, unlike anything she had ever seen on a beggar before. The sleeves were rolled to the elbow, revealing huge forearms. Around one wrist was tied a dirty red string.

"Where did you get that shirt?" she asked, unable to disguise her curiosity. "I have never seen anything like it."

"It is the work of many hands," said the man. "Like most things in this world. It is a gift from those who love me."

"If you are so loved," she replied, "then why must you beg on the streets?"

"Shush!" said her dueña. "Do not speak to him!"

The man held his hand up to the dueña, holding her off. "Because it is my lot in life," he answered. "I do not just take from people. I give back."

"Give back what?" asked the girl.

"I give people back their dreams."

"And do dreams get lost?"

"Oh yes," he said, "often."

"Very well," she said. "Nana, give the man some alms."

"But in your case," the man said, "a kiss will do."

"What insolence!" said the dueña.

But La Princesa, who was fearless, more so than her mother would wish, replied, "And what will happen? Will you turn into a handsome prince?"

"Oh, no, Princesa, never that. But I may become your hero someday."

"Will you find my dreams for me?" she asked.

"Perhaps. But you have not yet lost them."

"Very well," she replied, and over the noisy objections of her dueña, the girl stooped and kissed the man on his grimy forehead.

"Bless you," he said, "I will not forget," and cleared the way for them.

The dueña was much scandalized by this behavior, and only with the promise of exemplary behavior for all of the remainder of Lent did the girl keep the woman from telling her mother.

As the oldest of her family, La Princesa, as she was called by both her family and friends, was allowed certain privileges. Her younger brothers and sisters complained that she was the most beloved by their father. This, of course, he denied, but it was clear that the precocious daughter was much indulged. Tutored at home from an early age, she had quickly learned all there was to know, as far as she was concerned, to be a proper lady in Mexico, and she yearned to know more. Her mother was adamant that she not attend the university, where she would be exposed to all sorts of questionable elements, but there was some talk of sending her to Europe for finishing. This both excited and frightened her, and a decision had been postponed for the time being.

In the meantime, she visited the homes of her friends, some of them already married, attended certain parties with her parents, and planned for her fifteenth birthday, when she would be officially presented to society. And when no one was paying attention, she sat in her father's private study and paged through his medical texts, wondering when her life would begin.

✱

Increasingly, Noé found that the ideas to which he had been exposed at La Escuelita and in La Señorita's salon put him at odds with many of his instructors at the university.

"Sir," he said at the end of one especially egregious lecture on man and civilization, "you have the sensibilities of a jackass." And he left the class never to return.

This sort of behavior earned him a reputation among his classmates, one that he felt obligated to uphold. Eventually he stopped attending classes altogether, preferring the life of a journalist that was afforded to him by both his experience with his mother's endeavors and his own inclinations. In addition, since the day he had followed his mother to the Monte de Piedad, Noé had felt guilty about his schooling, yet had been unable to broach the subject of his tuition with his mother. He felt that she would be embarrassed by his knowledge. Thus, he announced that a formal education was of no further use to him and that he would seek regular employment with one of the many publications in the city.

"Is that wise?" asked his mother.

"I do not know, Mamá," he answered, "but I feel that I know as much as my professors at this point."

"Yes, but I suspect that they have learned much through experience and through virtue of their longer lives."

"Then I will live my life," Noé said simply, "and have experiences."

He could not be persuaded otherwise, and Estela found it hard to argue with Noé when he began to earn enough to sustain himself. Soon he announced that he would rent living quarters with his friend Samuel.

"But why?" asked Estela. "When you can continue to live here with us, where you do not need to pay rent?" She turned to La Señorita in exasperation and saw a surprising expression on her face. "With your permission, of course," she added.

"Let him go," said La Señorita. "He does not want to be surrounded by old women all of his life. Of course," she added, "he knows that he always has a home with me."

Had his apartment-mate not been of a family whom Estela trusted, she might not have agreed, but she did so reluctantly. She knew that Samuel, who was still a university student, would be a moderating influence on her willful son.

"It will be good for him," La Señorita assured her. "A young man must find his own way."

And find it he did, among the bodegas, the salons, the police stations, and the public gathering places of Mexico. Noé reveled in the tumultuous noise of the streets, the lurid details of petty crimes, in ferreting out the confessions of the more churlish of Mexico's residents. All of his life, he had been on a first-name basis with some of the baser elements of the city, through the women who came and went through the portals of La Paciencia. These women now served as his confidantes throughout the city, whether they were respectably employed or married, or back in the cantinas and boardinghouses where they had formerly plied their trades. They gave him fruit from their stands in the mercado, along with tidbits of information about the latest scandal.

Often Noé was the first to break a story, and his colleagues in the press marveled at his indefatigability. More than once, he and a colleague or two were picked up and taken to what was called the Writers' Salon at Belem, the penitentiary. This was a well-appointed holding cell at the top of the building, where they were questioned in a cordial manner over incidents covered in their various news accounts. A little plata in the right hands usually secured their release, though on at least one occasion, Noé had spent the night for emphasis.

On occasion, in more respectable settings, he ran into the young woman whom he had discovered was called La Princesa not just by himself but by all who knew her. She could be found in the company of her dueña, when she was distant and demure, or in the company of other young women of the better families, when she was much bolder. They could sometimes be found in the Alameda on Sunday afternoons, dressed like a flock of birds for the outing, birds with hats and parasols.

"Who are you, really?" she asked him mischievously one day, when he had been trying to impress her with his knowledge of the events of the times. "Your mother's son, or"—here she shot him a challenging look—"your father's?"

He was not sure how much she might know about him. Chances were, not very much. Still, her question made him giddy with the possibilities that it offered. "I am my own person," he replied, "sprung directly from the head of Chronos, a child of my times."

"And what does that mean?" she came back. "A child subject to the whims of time? Or a child who will shape his time?"

"We are all the subjects of time, my princesa, even you, whose principality, or should I say, whose princessipality, resides, by necessity, within it. But I have chosen to be a chronicler of my time, thus, both son and father to my times."

"Not both father and mother, as well as son?"

"Perhaps that, too, since I have written under a multitude of names, both fathers' names and mothers' names. You could say, perhaps, that my name is Legion."

"I have suspected that for some time," she replied with a smile.

"Then why have you not called me by name?"

"Should I call you Father Time or Mother Nature? A sister or a brother? Or merely a son of a mother's son? Or should I invoke him whose name darkens the dreams of the sinful?"

"I don't claim such powers. Merely the common will of the masses whose sentiments see the light through my writings. Again, I am probably all of these things, though I do not feel very sisterly to you, but for convenience sake, you may address me as Noé, a su servicio."

"Very well, Noé, arise and take your place in time."

"And you? Must I address you by your royal title forever?"

"For now it pleases me."

"Then it pleases me as well, and I will do as you wish."

"I do wish. And I must go now. Adieu, Noé."

"Adieu, mademoiselle."

Noé watched her go from the Alameda with her friends, giggling and whispering.

"You know who she is, don't you?" asked Samuel, who had observed this exchange with some amusement.

"Don't tell me," replied Noé. "I would rather wait until she chooses to tell me herself. Besides, if I knew the truth, I might lose all nerve. I am sure that she is far above me in her station, and that I would lose all hope if I were to know just how far."

"Very well," said Samuel. "Though a difference in stations was not what I had in mind."

"Still," said Noé, "I prefer the bliss of my ignorance to the hard reality of truth." He stopped. "I'm not related to her, am I?"

"No," replied Samuel, giving him a pained smile. "I hope not."

After that, Noé managed to encounter La Princesa on a regular basis. While never without her dueña or friends, La Princesa managed to go skating on a regular basis at El Tivolí, where Noé could also be found. At the late-afternoon intersection between the ladies' skate and the open skate, where Noé waited outside the rink with a carreta to transport L'Orchestre back to their quarters, they were able to exchange a little banter now and then.

"Noé," she would say solemnly, "is my transport ready?"

"Absolutely, my princesa," he would reply, making a sweeping gesture towards the open cart, its skinny mule held by a bored mozo, as though it were a bejeweled and canopied carriage. "It awaits your command, to take you to your palace in the city, or your retreat in the mountains, along the shore of your crystalline lake."

"Very well," she would reply, "my ladies in waiting will arrive shortly."

And the women of L'Orchestre would emerge from El Tivolí, hand up their musical instruments, hike up their skirts, and clamber onto the wagon. They could never understand why there was a group of giggling girls nearby, but suspected that it had something to do with Noé.

"Ah, Noé," said El Profesor sometimes, "does your mother know that you are flirting with half of Mexico City when you are supposed to be helping?"

"I am always helping the women of Mexico," Noé would answer. "Some of them need one kind of help, and some of them need another. I am merely paying them the attention that they deserve."

✶

When Estela entered the courtyard of La Paciencia, she saw the crowd that gathered around anything unusual. In this case, she saw that it was a visit from Beto, the mysterious Opata from the north who graced them with his presence now and then. What was different this time was that La Señorita was one of those gathered about him. Her visits to the school, seldom enough, were never accidental, and it filled Estela with unease to see the two of them together. It put her in mind of portents and omens, blue moons and two-headed calves.

As she approached them, Beto stared at her with an appraising look.

"What do you see?" she asked. Her years in the Capital had made her bold.

"I see that you are unlucky in love."

"That is the past," she answered. "Tell me what the future holds."

"The future holds . . . itself. It is like a rawhide bag, with us like stones within it. Only we cannot tell where we will be cast out."

"So now I am not only unlucky in love, but hard as a stone as well?"

"Stones are resilient," said La Señorita. "They stand the test of time."

"In Casas Grandes," said Beto, "there is a stone that has been dressed in cotton and feathers and treated as a holy object. That stone is wiser than all of us, having fallen from heaven."

Estela looked at Beto, again wondering just how much he knew about her. "I feel like Mother Time," she said, seating herself on a bench and removing her hat. "I feel as though I have been here a long time." She sat and fanned herself.

Beto and La Señorita continued to regard her, Beto seated on a mat on the ground, La Señorita standing beside him. They looked like a pair of gargoyles.

"What is it?" asked Estela impatiently.

"There has been an earthquake in the north," said La Señorita. "In Texas, the sea rushed in and inundated the port of Galveston."

"The church in Bacanori, Sonora, has collapsed," said Beto. "I saw it fall last night. Many things have shifted and changed."

"And Saltillo?" asked Estela, standing now. "Did anything happen there?"

"I do not know," said La Señorita. "Many of the telegraph lines are disrupted. Perhaps they are safe."

Beto shrugged. "Perhaps not."

Estela stood. "I will send word to Noé. He will be able to find out."

✱

Noé came that evening to the house on Bucareli Street. "No one knows," he said. "Reports are coming in from all over, but very slowly. It seems that the earthquake was confined just to the north."

"What if my family is dead?" said Estela. "My children?"

This seemed odd to Noé, since he was not aware that his mother had even written to her other children since she had left. Perhaps she received letters he did not know about. Nevertheless, he knew that the past had weighed on her of late, as though she had some foreknowledge of disaster. "Perhaps you should return," he said.

"The roads will be bad," said La Señorita. "They always are after a misfortune. And the bandits will be out, to take advantage of the victims."

"Well then, I will go with you," said Noé. "Besides, I remember nothing. Isn't it time that you showed me the place of my birth?"

Estela looked at him as though he were a total stranger. It was true. It had never occurred to her that Noé would not remember Saltillo. He was a citizen of the Capital, through and through.

"You are right," she said. "You would not remember your sisters."

Noé knew that he had a brother, too, but his mother never spoke of him. There was so much, he thought, of which she never spoke.

M Cardoz had another secret in his heart. Every night his heart spoke to him. He did not understand what it was trying to say. It knocked loudly at the inside of his chest, so loudly that he feared that it would wake his wife, sleeping gently beside him.

During these odd and sleepless nights, M Cardoz had time to think. He had spent many years reading history and philosophy while waiting for worthy projects to be brought to his small shop, and from his studies, he determined that most men strove, above all, to leave behind them an immortal reputation. Even the most gifted, the Roman emperors and Greek poets, the Spanish jurisconsults and Italian artists, had the future in mind. For this, they constructed statues and monuments and hoped to have many speeches made about their worthy and admirable traits. They wrote books and painted pictures and praised the beauty of women not because women were beautiful—which, of course, they were—but because the flatterers hoped to be remembered for their dulcet words.

Even those who left behind bad reputations—pirates and dictators, murderers and confidence men—did so in the form of horrible stories and broken hearts and bad debts. They sacked cities and tortured the innocent and stole from the worthy, not because they desired ruined towns or broken bodies or ill-gotten gold, but because they hoped to be remembered for their ill deeds. In other words, the world was cluttered with reputations, both good and bad.

One night, M Cardoz realized what his heart was trying to tell him. It was that, although he appeared to be a vigorous man at the prime of his life, his heart was knocking itself to pieces, and he was not long for this world.

From the moment that the printer realized his days were numbered, he began to arrange for all traces of himself to be obliterated. Unlike most men, who spend the greater part of their lives trying to memorialize themselves in death, M Cardoz wished to be forgotten. He was determined not to leave behind any reputation at all. Why should he, he thought, a mere transmitter of other people's words and images, leave a reputation? Having a reputation had not served his ancestors well. The rumor of tainted blood was simply one more thing they had had to flee in their quest for survival.

As his heart knocked more loudly to be released from the earthly confinement of his ribs, and he began to wheeze with fatigue from the mere exertion of raising himself to a standing position, M Cardoz began to dismantle every sign of his existence in this world. To that end, the front pages of books bearing his imprint were removed, and he sent his wife to begin erasing his name from official documents.

This unusual request did not come as a surprise to his wife and children. It seemed merely to be an extension of the trajectory of his life, his philosophical leanings, and a fulfillment of the lives of his long and purposefully colorless family. The habit of using an initial instead of a first name had begun at least two hundred years earlier, and part of the last name was already missing. It was natural that, at some point, the name should be obliterated altogether.

During M Cardoz' last night on earth, his heart told him that things were getting worse in Mexico. Already, it reminded him, many of his clients had been jailed or died under mysterious circumstances. Others had published statements retracting the things they had published in earlier times. People had begun to look more furtive, more harried when they appeared at his shop, and some said that they feared they had been followed. This forced him to move his shop more often, sometimes more than once in a week.

His heart beat and beat and told him that great tragedy would soon overtake the city. Many lives would be lost. Years of famine and disorder would follow, and the poor would be pitted against the rich. Mexico would be plunged into hopeless debt to the foreign investors who had been so carefully cultivated. In building a reputation, Don Porfírio was in the process of ruining the country.

Cardoz whispered to his wife that, in addition to his other instructions, the family must leave Mexico as soon as possible. If they wanted, they could return in twenty years' time. His wife, to this point, had been very brave and had hidden her tears from him. But this last instruction, that she must leave all that she had ever known and live in a strange land, was more than she could bear. She was certain that she would not live long enough to return to and die in her beloved Mexico. But as with his other requests, she felt that she could not refuse him. He had always been a good man and had done everything in his power to give his family a quiet, secure life. He had never been frivolous or nervous, and would not ask this of her if he did not feel it was necessary.

At dawn, M Cardoz was calm. He had been awakened by the tiniest of tremors, a mere vibration that someone not so attuned to his inner workings would never have noticed. It was the slightest shifting in the foundation, a mere splash in the water table far below the surface of the earth. It was a puff of wind setting the butterflies to flight, the displacement of warm air with cold far to the north. He felt that the final times had begun, the events that his heart had described to him. His heart gave a final surge, and then burst. It flooded his chest and carried him away on the tide of his own blood. His last sensation was of being thrust out to sea in a small boat, with no horizon ahead, and the light playing gently on the blue and tremulous water all around him.

The day of his funeral, the widow Cardoz and her children laid the printer to rest under a beautiful stone that bore no name at all, only the chiseled image of an open book, its pages blank. He was interred in a special part of a special cemetery, and as they had been bidden, his family took up life under a new name.

Much to their sorrow, the family began to sell off their things, pack a few possessions, and prepare to migrate. His wife ran her hand along the rim of a huge blue urn in their courtyard and wondered if she could take it with her. Its interior was the natural dark red of the fired earth. The vase had been purchased by her grandmother, who said that it was the exact blue of the Mediterranean Sea in her land of birth. Their friends and acquaintances assumed that the printer had left debts that needed to be repaid, but they were merely following his instructions. The printer had, in fact, left them well off, having saved carefully for the vagaries of life, just as his forebearers had done.

The ancient press was dismantled, the plates broken and scattered, and the shop bearing the name M Cardoz never appeared again. It took people years to believe that it had disappeared for good. They were always certain that they would find it just around the next corner. In the select books and periodicals that had been printed on the ancient and curious press, his name mysteriously disappeared, as though fixed in invisible ink that was guaranteed to fade away after a certain length of time. The rest of the publication remained intact, so that it appeared to have been printed anonymously.

With the printer's death, *La Linterna* ceased publication because La Señorita would trust no one else with its special mission. The copies in existence were passed from hand to hand and became dog-eared with constant perusal. A few women were able to learn the pamphlets by heart and could recite the words and a description of the pictures upon prompting. This they were asked to do in sewing circles, on lonely and disreputable street corners, at the edge of the canal, where clothing was scrubbed clean, and in the fields outside of the city when the women paused for a moment to rest from their unceasing labors.

M Cardoz knew that this, in the end, would be his legacy. The many people he had reached, the ideas of freedom and education, of practical advice and common wisdom that had been passed from hand to hand, from mouth to ear, from city to field and university to jacal, were there due to his ceaseless labor. Although his name would be forgotten, his family and belongings scattered, the ideas he helped to perpetuate would live on. The seeds of human dignity had been planted and were not easily stamped out.

WHY DO YOU CRY, MI REINA?

I t was a gloomy day. The sky, uncharacteristically, was overcast, the air heavy with humidity. La Princesa strolled, unaccompanied. She held a pair of roller skates over one shoulder in a desultory fashion, kicking at the ground with her fine kid boots. She bit her lips and tears came, unbidden, to her eyes.

"Why do you cry, mi reina?"

The question came unexpectedly, a harsh, grating sound. She looked into a passageway to see the strange man with no legs, the one whom she had kissed. His embroidered shirt glowed brightly as he came forward out of the shadows.

"My papá wants to send me away."

"Away? Where?"

"To Europe. He thinks that I could benefit from the atmosphere."

"And is there a better atmosphere in Europe than in Mexico?"

"I don't see how there could be any finer atmosphere. If I have to go, I will die. I will wither away from loneliness."

"But you are young, Princesa. The young seldom wither away of loneliness, no matter where they are."

"But I will. I will be the first."

"Is it loneliness that you will die of, or is it perhaps something else?"

"I do not understand what you mean."

"Is it, perhaps, love?"

"I don't think so, but there is someone I will miss terribly."

"A young man?"

She smiled slightly through her tears, not answering. Her eyes were fixed on the ground, but she did not make any motion to move on.

"Aha. I see that it is."

"Oh, but it is not really love," she protested. "He is merely a friend. It is just that he . . ." Here she stopped and looked away into the distance, as though searching for the answer. "He talks to me as though I am a real person. He talks about books and politics, as though I will understand. No one has ever treated me that way before."

"And yet I see that you are treated royally."

"Oh, I know I have everything. You must think me a fool. But my parents see me as"—she kicked at the ground—"a girl."

"A girl rather than a person?"

"Yes."

"A girl who should think about girl things?"

"Exactly! My father says that politics are a man's affair, that I should not bother about such things."

"And why do you?"

"Because it is important! Noé—I mean my friend—says that the men who run Mexico are ruining it and must be stopped."

"And what would you do?"

"Oh, I don't know. Perhaps try to convince others."

"Like your father?"

"My father is a doctor. He is not a politician."

"They say Los Cientificos, Don Porfírio's advisers, are doctors and learned men, not just politicians. And perhaps your father knows some of those learned men."

"Yes."

"And you have tried to talk to him."

"Yes," she whispered.

"There are great changes in the air," said Beto. "Many people are talking about them."

"I feel that Mexico has a great future," said La Princesa. "A Mexican future, not a European one. What do I care about Paris? I am afraid that I will miss everything."

"You will not miss everything. Remember your dreams."

"That's right. You said that you could find people's dreams."

"I can."

"Can you help me to stay in Mexico?"

Beto did not answer right away. He sat and stared at the young girl, now becoming a woman. "I could, but everything in this world costs."

"You mean money? I have . . ." She hesitated. "I could obtain . . . a little."

"No, I do not need money. But I could give you a gift. It would be an expensive gift, a terrible gift."

"How could a gift be terrible?" she asked.

"When you accept an important gift from someone, among my people, you are bound to them. It begins a relationship that lasts forever, and you must fulfill this obligation for the rest of your life. When we are born, we have this obligation to the land of our birth. If I gave you such a gift, it would bind you to Mexico forever. Do you wish to have this gift? Would you accept such an obligation?"

"Oh, yes," she said. "I would take such an obligation."

"Then do as I say," said Beto. "Tomorrow, go to the home of La Señorita Mejora de Gonga and say that I have sent you. Say that you are willing to do whatever is required of you by La Señorita." He held up his hand when she began to speak. "But you must think about this tonight. You must consider it very carefully, because once you accept, there will be no turning back. You may be required to give up everything that you have known and loved. You may be required to give up your family, and even your special friend. Do you understand?"

"Yes," she said. "I think I do." And once again she stooped and kissed him. "Thank you."

Beto gazed into her eyes. "Don't forget," he said, leaning towards her, "that underneath this beautiful shirt is a very ugly body. But a body, nevertheless."

La Princesa broke his gaze and practically ran home, where her dueña, frantic with worry, was waiting. She had been with friends, said La Princesa, with girlfriends from the afternoon skate at El Tivolí.

"You will be the death of me," said the dueña, seating herself on a couch with her fan working vigorously. "What will people think? Now change into something decent before your father returns. Don't let him see you in that outrageous getup."

La Princesa went to her room to change from the bloomer-like outfit she wore for skating into a more sedate dress.

✳

At dinner she made one last plea to remain in Mexico. "Please, Papá. Let me stay. I could find something productive to do."

Carranza deliberately chewed a mouthful of food and took a sip of wine. "Like what?" he asked.

She thought a moment. "I could assist you in your surgery."

"Absolutely not," said her mother. "I wouldn't think of allowing you to do something like that. The only productive thing you could possibly do in Mexico would be to marry. And you refuse to even see the young men who come to call on you." La Señora Carranza looked like a ruffled guinea fowl at the end of the table.

"Your mother has spoken," said Carranza. "I don't see how I can contradict her."

She tried again. "What about your charity work? And that of Mamá?"

"When you are a respectable married woman," her mother said severely, "then you can do charitable work. But until then, it is not appropriate to associate with . . . the less fortunate."

She opened her mouth, many things wanting to come out, then shut it again. Carranza said nothing.

La Princesa began to feel the tears well up in her eyes again. "You just want to be rid of me," she said.

"Not at all," said her father. He waved his fork in the air. "Someday all this will be yours."

"Assuming you marry well," added her mother.

"What about me?" asked her brother, who had remained silent up to this point.

"Oh, your father was only joking," said La Señora. "Of course you and your brother will inherit. Your sister must simply marry well."

"Yes," said her father. He seemed in an especially jovial mood. "Why don't you bring us a prince from the Continent? After all, your mother knows that the men of Mexico are no good."

His wife gave him a cool look.

La Princesa began to weep openly. "Why do you mock me?" she cried. "I don't want a prince from the Continent. I only want to stay here."

"Oh, please excuse yourself from the table," said her mother, "and allow the rest of us to eat in peace. We only have your best interests in mind. We will discuss this at a later time. Nothing has to be decided this instant."

She continued to sit at the table and weep.

"Do as your mother says," said Carranza, his voice rising, his mood suddenly changed, "if you wish to receive any consideration at all from us."

La Princesa fled the table. In her room, surrounded by dolls dressed in lace, she contemplated herself in the mirror. What could the froglike man have meant? She did not even know his name. How could she tell La Señorita, of whom she had heard, that he had sent her? Did he really mean that she must go the next day? How would she get away from her dueña again? La Princesa felt unequal to the task that had been set for her, yet she realized that the longer she hesitated, the more likely that she would be sent away. She had much to ponder that night.

TREASURES IN HEAVEN

I am falling apart with yearning for things that I never knew," Noé said to his mother. "The first birds of spring, the clear rush of water down a mountainside I have never seen.

"Where are these things? Who has told me of them? They are in the place of my birth, and while you have not spoken these things out loud, I have seen them in your eyes, and in the moving hands of my nona as she tends her garden. They have passed like a moth upon the lips of my grandfather, and lighted in your eyes as you gaze out the window, drinking your coffee.

"We must go back—if not for my sake, then for yours."

✳

Estela lifted the heavy knocker and dropped it once, then again, against the door. No one came, although she could hear the sounds of everyday life going on elsewhere in the house—running water, someone humming absentmindedly and walking about while performing a mindless task, and very faintly, chickens making their contented noises in the back garden. Sounds that she recognized. Sounds that, altogether, made a home.

She called her sister's name. "Blanca? Blanca!"

A man's voice called out, "Viola? Viola! There is someone at the door!" Receiving no answer, he came grumbling to the door himself. He was an older man in his shirtsleeves, as though home for the day.

"Bueno?" he asked.

Estela tried to make out who he could be. His hair was grey, and his shirt tight around his bulging waist.

"Gustavo?" she asked.

He looked long and hard at her, not able to place who she might be.

"Yes, Gustavo Ochoa Cardenas, at your service."

"Is Blanca in? It is her sister."

She watched his face change again, from confusion to skepticism.

"Estela?"

"Please, is Blanca in?"

"Please come in," he said. But he was still formal with her, disbelieving. "I will go and see if she is available."

Estela entered the little passageway that opened at its other end into the courtyard. It was so peaceful there, in the old house where they had grown up. She placed her things on a low bench and ventured forward to look at the flowers.

Gustavo was gone for some time. At last he returned. "My wife, Blanca, says that her sister Estela left years ago, went to Mexico City, and has not come back. She says that you cannot be Estela."

"Gustavo!" she exclaimed. She did not know what to say. "Don't you think she would recognize me, her own sister? Don't you recognize me?"

He peered at her again, then fumbled in his pockets for something. "I'm sorry, I can't find my glasses. My eyes are bad now, you know, and I can't really be sure," he said apologetically. "And it has been—how long? Many years."

"Seventeen years," Estela said. She moved dreamily to the edge of the garden, as though she was only half aware of his presence. "Andale," she said. "Go and get her."

Again Gustavo disappeared down the long galleria towards a back room, where Estela could hear muffled voices—first his, then hers, as they debated the possibilities of such a return.

"I am so sorry," he said, emerging sometime later. "My wife— I mean to say Blanca—says that her sister must be dead after all these years. She has not written in at least fifteen years. Why would she—you—come to visit without writing?"

Estela listened to caged finches singing in the courtyard. "I have not written because I had too much to say," answered Estela, folding and refolding her gloves in her hands. "Things that would not fit into letters. They were too big."

Gustavo seemed at a loss as to what to do with that information.

"How are the children?" asked Estela.

"Well, they are fine," said Gustavo. "They are grown up, and well. All but the youngest two are married, with children of their own." He shrugged helplessly. This was a conversation his wife should be having. He was not used to discussing his children with a strange woman.

"I came because I heard that there was an earthquake, a flood. I came to check on my daughters," said Estela, turning suddenly, looking at him. "How are they? María, Victoria?"

Gustavo stood with his mouth partly open. "Just a minute," he said, "I will try to get her to come out," and disappeared again.

Estela paced off the little passageway, humming to herself. She did not know where her daughters lived now. She could not yet admit to herself that she had lost her way, trying to find her own house. The main streets had been changed, widened, and the mercado was no longer at the same corner. She had seen no evidence of recent damage from an earthquake, just the old scars of time and the military invasion from the United States, things that had been there since her childhood.

Again she heard their voices in the back and wondered if Blanca was well. Perhaps she could not get up, or was permanently bedridden. Estela's own ankle began to hurt, recalling her injury long ago, when she had first met Victor. She had walked a long way today, not wanting to engage a carriage, but preferring the memories brought back by the rough, cobbled streets. It was here that she had first met Victor Carranza, turning her ankle in the street.

She began to gather up her things, not sure that this had been a good idea after all, and prepared to leave, when Gustavo returned. His step sounded a little more confident this time. Estela sensed a plan.

"All right," he said, sounding more like his old self. "She, Blanca, says to ask you a question. If you know the answer to this question, then she will believe that you are her sister and will come out to see you."

"Bueno," she said. "What is the question?"

"She asks, what was her nickname when she was a child? Her sister called her by a special name. What was she called?"

Estela's mind went back, back to those times before either of them had children, before their twin brother and sister were born, when they were younger than blossoms, younger than baby birds, when the whole world was new. She breathed in the air of the garden, the same garden where they had nursed their dolls when their mother was alive, and played with the twins when she was gone. It seemed like such a long time, longer than people should have to live.

"She was called Negra. I called her La Negra." Her voice was firm, certain.

Gustavo looked skeptical, but went away with this bit of knowledge.

In a minute, Blanca came hobbling down the hall, leaning on a stick. "Is that you? Estela, is that you?"

They fell into each other's arms, weeping, before collapsing onto the bench among Estela's shawl and gloves and the other things that she carried in a small satchel. Blanca was heavy and her hair thinner, but otherwise she looked well. After assuring himself that the two women wanted to be with each other, Gustavo disappeared a final time.

"How could it be you? How could it be you?" Blanca exclaimed over and over again. They were both tearful and smiling.

"It is me. Bless me, it is me," said Estela, equally overcome.

The maid returned with some shopping, and Blanca called for her to fix them a little sustenance before they both died of hunger.

"You are so thin!" she said to Estela. "Don't you eat? Doesn't that man feed you?" She stopped herself, as Estela looked down, blushing. She could imagine what people had thought all these years.

"I . . . I live by myself," she stammered. "Una soltera."

Blanca looked unbelieving.

"I live at the home of the woman I work for, La Señorita Mejora de la Gonga. She employs me to run a school for women and children, a charity."

"Ah," said Blanca. She rose, with difficulty, as the maid returned. It took both Estela and the maid to balance her on her cane.

"My feet have gotten worse and worse," she said. "The doctor says it is gout."

Estela noticed that Blanca wore loose slippers on her feet, which were wide and swollen, more swollen than mere overweight would account for.

The maid led them to a wrought-iron table in the courtyard, similar to, if not the same table that Estela used to sit at every single day when she lived in Saltillo. She used to join her sister each afternoon for merienda even after they were both grown with families of their own. Now there were pecan cookies, fruit, and manzanillo tea waiting for them. One bite of a cookie and Estela nearly swooned with the accumulated weight of her memories.

"So," said Blanca, patting her on the hand. "Tell me everything. From the beginning. Tell me everything."

Estela did not know where to begin, what to say, so she did as she was asked and started at the beginning.

✷

After a while, Noé was shown into the courtyard, and Estela saw him with her sister's eyes, a tall young man, holding his hat shyly in his hands. She had sent him with their trunk to find rooms for them. Estela watched her sister's face.

Blanca looked and looked, then put her hand to her cheek as she was introduced. "Noé?" she said, then looked at Estela and back to Noé. "But . . . but you look exactly like . . . Zacarías!"

Estela could not help but roll her eyes. They had all seen Noé when he was born. Nevertheless, they must have thought that she had gone to Mexico City to raise Victor's son near him. She saw how rumors, like weeds, grow up over and then overwhelm the truth. And after a few years, rumor becomes the truth.

Noé smiled graciously as he was seated, which was good, since he would probably have to go through this a few more times.

"But you must stay here!" said Blanca. "Go and fetch your things. You cannot stay at an inn when you have family here!"

And so Noé was sent out into the street again, barely having had a chance to drink a cup of tea.

By now Blanca had two maids scurrying back and forth, preparing a feast and sending out messages. She managed all this without leaving her seat at the table. As the afternoon lengthened, Estela put on her shawl, and Blanca had one brought out for herself.

People began to show up, one by one, smiling young women who looked like Blanca and Gustavo, and giggling children who had come to see the exotic aunt from Mexico City. Noé returned with the trunk and stood and sat politely as was required of him, until Blanca's youngest, a schoolteacher a little younger than Noé, returned. Then Noé joined him on the street to smoke. He and his one unmarried sister still lived at home with their parents. The house and courtyard began to fill up with women talking excitedly, children running and playing.

A feast was laid out under the portico, tables placed end to end, and candles were lit along the way. Gustavo re-emerged dressed for dinner, his glasses fastened securely to his face, and this time he greeted Estela heartily, like a brother-in-law should. The young husbands began to show up, one by one, as they returned from work and were informed of the goings-on, and Noé had found a place among the giggling cousins, who were pelting him with questions about the Capital.

And then the woman with her mother's sad eyes came in, accompanied by her daughter.

Estela stood and embraced her daughter Victoria, wordlessly, tears streaming down her face. Victoria was dressed in black. Her young soldier husband had been killed within a year of their marriage, leaving Victoria with their one daughter. She rented out rooms in the house that had once been Estela's, living quietly and frugally in the one section she kept for herself. Her own daughter was now married and had come with her mother on this occasion, to meet her grandmother Estela.

Tears rained down like birds, but the hurts were all old— old wounds that had been given time to heal. There was no

anger, no recriminations of death, abandonment, scandal.
They had all lived with these things for too long a time.

They ate. Noé looked and wondered at these people, the rest
of his family, whom he had never met. He watched them
surreptitiously, looking for signs of resemblance, and they
watched him more openly, the acknowledged novelty of the
evening. Noé wondered at their lives here, so far from the
Capital, where news must reach them like rumor and innu-
endo, as fitfully and unpredictably as the weather.

He admitted that he was a journalist, and Gustavo, now
retired, with two of his sons running the business, launched
into his views on the state of the world. Noé was used to this,
and welcomed the familiar topics with enthusiasm.

After listening to his views on the economy, Gustavo said,
"You speak well. I can see why you have become a writer."

"I learned from my mother and grandparents," he said, nodding to Estela at the far end of the table, near her sister. "They
taught me early to know the value of the good word."

This brought a brief lull—of confusion from the younger
people, embarrassment from the older—at the memory of Noé's
paternal grandparents, who had been driven from Saltillo by
a mob. Noé could hear the word *judíos* being whispered and
repeated between cousins. Could Noé possibly know this part
of their history?

Gustavo cleared his throat. "You must think us barbarians
out here, for what happened to them," he said. "But those were
confused and dangerous times."

"I see barbarism every day in the Capital," said Noé, "against
the poor. I do not think that people can be too different here."

This seemed to reassure everyone, and all began talking
again. Nevertheless, the unspoken question of the fate of Noé's
father hung, like a banner of smoke, in the air.

As it grew dark, the young families began to excuse themselves, one by one. Sleepy children were draped over shoulders, and the men stopped to shake Noé's hand as they filed
out. He was exhausted from meeting so many strangers. Noé
stepped up behind his mother, and when she turned, he realized that he had never seen her so happy, her sister on one side,
her daughter on the other. Nor had he realized how much older
she had become, until this moment, the dark shadows now
permanent around her eyes, her thick, chestnut hair streaked
with white.

"I'm going to bed now," he said.

"Go, go," she said. "I will in a little while."

As he walked down the corridor to the bedroom that had
been cleared for him, Noé thought that, perhaps, his mother
should stay here with her family, here where people knew her
as more than La Viuda Carabajál.

The next day they went to visit María.

Estela's older daughter had entered the convent shortly
after her mother left for Mexico City. The older, unmarried
sister of a younger married woman, her parents gone, María
felt that she had no choice. But she also had not had a novio,
so it was not a difficult choice. The order had been happy to
take her, and her decision had been seen, in part, as a concil-
iatory gesture on the part of the family towards the Catholic
Church for all the scandal that had been caused. Her grandfather Don Horacio had paid her dowry, knowing that it would
have pleased his deceased wife, Altagracia.

For María, the convent had been something of a relief. Her
last year before taking the veil had been fraught with too much
anxiety and decision-making. Many of the household duties
had fallen on her shoulders as her mother pursued her own

concerns, and María had especially worried over Victoria's nocturnal absences.

She had not told her mother, although she knew Victoria was slipping out to see someone, for fear of the consequences for both of them. This was when she, too, had hoped to meet a husband, and feared that punishment to Victoria would fall upon her as well. Guilt had taken its toll.

María welcomed the release of her independence to become a bride of Christ. She rose before dawn to attend prayers. Every morning for seven years, she had cleaned the stables where milk cows were kept. For the next seven years she had washed all the floors of the convent on her hands and knees. Recently she had been allowed to learn how to process the fine cheese that the convent made for sale to the community and that constituted part of its livelihood.

She was allowed to meet her mother and brother in a small room near the entrance to the convent, furnished with a single chair. Other than her sister Victoria, no one had come to see María in years. Estela tried to get her to sit in the chair, but she insisted on standing.

"I am used to it," she said, without rancor.

Estela petted the rough hands, barely recognizable as those of a woman, so worn were they by hard work. María could hardly endure the touch, and soon withdrew her hands into the depths of her habit. She and Noé acknowledged each other as strangers do, nodding politely. A great cedar tree moved in a breeze outside, alternately casting the small room in sun and in shadow. Although they were not far outside of town, the convent seemed in a distant country. Estela marveled at how quiet it was, how different from the former cloister in Mexico City where she had spent so much time over the last years, a place filled with the lusty sounds of life being reclaimed. Here, breathing gently with the trees, life seemed to be suppressed, without being snuffed out completely.

Estela tried to look into her daughter's eyes, searching for signs of love, or hate, or yearning. She had no idea, when she left, that her older daughter would go into a convent, though it was not unheard of. She wondered at her younger self for abandoning the young girl to such a fate. María, both of her daughters, had been so lively.

"I'm sorry," she said, simply.

"There's no need," said María. "God has sufficed. He will reward me in heaven."

Estela, looking into the remote eyes of her daughter, could see what it had cost her.

Then Estela's eyes widened. She recognized the echo of Gloria Quinque's words about women sacrificing themselves in this life for the diaphanous promise of treasures in the next. It was from this passive condition, not from the streets, that Estela had worked so hard to save the women of La Paciencia. And she realized that in saving them, for her own selfish reasons, she had lost her own daughter. This hurt more than any betrayal she had ever known.

✱

Estela and Noé boarded the carriage that would take them back to Blanca and Gustavo's without a word. Estela was drawn deep into herself, overwhelmed with memories and guilt. Noé, twelve days out of Mexico City, was already restless.

"What do you think?" said Estela finally. "Are we better off living as saints in this life so as to gain treasures in heaven?"

Noé thought for a moment. "My grandfather would say that every day is a pearl, that the laughter of a child is more precious than gold."

Noé looked at his mother and saw the devastation in her face.

"I think that you should stay here," said Noé, after a bit.

Estela did not answer at first, only sighed. "I have my work."

"Hermelinda can do it," said Noé, "and Corona. La Señorita does not lack for resources."

Estela said nothing.

"Besides," said Noé, "it is going to get dangerous."

"But why?" asked Estela, actually looking at him for perhaps the first time that day.

"Things are changing. Politically. Don Porfírio is taking stronger and stronger measures to suppress his opposition."

"All we do is help the poor. Surely he cannot object to that."

Even as she said it, Estela knew that what Noé said was true. The poor were his opposition. "Anyway, what can he do to us?"

"People have disappeared," said Noé. "Just because I go to prison and get released does not mean that others do."

"All the more reason for me to continue in Mexico City!" Estela exclaimed. "To make sure that you are safe! Unless," she said, glancing at him, "you intend to stay here as well."

"No," said Noé, "I cannot. I have my work!" he said, parroting his mother with a smile. "I left many things undone," he added mysteriously.

"So have I!" said Estela, sitting up suddenly, as though she had just remembered something.

"Mamá," said Noé, and drew a black velvet bag from his pocket, pressing it into her hands. "I thought about this before we left. I spoke with La Señorita. Everything is in order. You may stay if you wish. And I wish that you would."

Taking the bag from Noé, Estela opened it and drew out the sapphire necklace. She handled its fanciful gems, its impossibly ornate setting. She thought of broken dishes and chickens, of moonlit train rides and scandalous women, of Beto, of Mariana and Julio, and finally, of a single rose in a cut-glass vase, its petals touched on their tips with shameless red. Last of all, deep down in her heart's memory, yet fresh enough to make her catch her breath, Estela thought of Victoria and María and Gabriel as they once had been, and the life she'd led with Zacarías. It seemed so distant now, like the life of another person, told to her by a friend. Her hands begin to tremble, and tears, the tears she had been unable to shed for María, began to course down her face.

"Oh, Noé, how could you know . . ."

"I have known for some time," he said, "though not for long enough. I wish that you had told me. All those years, I wish that I had known," he said, sitting back in frustration.

"There was no reason to tell you," she said. "This necklace has served me well, although I have often wondered what my mother would have thought."

Noé shrugged and smiled at her. The very idea of Estela's mother—the woman Estela vaguely remembered from her youth, and the daguerreotype in the silver frame that was Noé's only concept of her—understanding the life she and Noé had led was absurd, and they both began to laugh.

"Andale, Mamá," said Noé. "Stay here with your family. I can have the rest of your things sent from México."

Estela was silent for a moment, looking out the window at the trees, the fields around them. "Very well," she said finally. "Only promise me one thing, you with the silver pen."

"What is that?"

"That you will write all of this down."

"All of what? The story of your life?"

"All of it." She waved her hand, encompassing the carriage, the road, the houses by the wayside, the two of them. And, Noé suspected, much more. "Just the way I tell it to you."

"Very well, Mamá. I will certainly try."

✶

Her return was not noted in the society column of the local paper.

✳

Before leaving Saltillo, Noé decided to take a walk. Following the directions and descriptions he had heard so many times— the cobblestone road, the house by the rushing stream, the bridge across to where the almond trees used to bloom—Noé made his way up the steep path to the top of the hill above Saltillo. All the way, he warned himself not to take what he saw too hard. He had heard the story of devastation as his grand-parents and his mother had told it, how they fled the house just before the arrival of the soldiers, the last time they saw their son, his father, Zacarías.

What he found instead surprised him.

Rather than an abandoned property given over to weeds and charred timber, Noé came upon a small, neatly kept house. Outside, two children played with a kitten, while a young man, not much older than himself, toiled at breaking up the hard soil in a vegetable garden.

"Hola," called Noé as he entered the small yard.

The man leaned upon his shovel, looking thankful for a break. "Hello," he answered. "May I help you?"

"I am visiting from Mexico City," answered Noé.

"That's wonderful!" said the man. "How is it there?"

The two children came running over to view the stranger.

"Well, times are interesting," said Noé, "as here."

"Amen," said the man. "How do you find our town?"

"Very beautiful," said Noé. "My parents were born here."

"Oh! So you are almost a native!" said the man.

"Well, I feel like a stranger. But I have wanted to visit for a long time."

"Come in," said the man. "And have something to drink. I am the Reverend Bernardo Castro. These are my children.

My wife has gone into town for a few things, but she will be back shortly."

As they walked towards the little house, Noé saw that there was a hand-lettered sign in a front window that said, CRISTO ES REY—Christ is King.

Castro invited Noé to be seated in the small front room, which was furnished with wooden benches pushed neatly against the walls. He brought him a glass of water.

"I was looking for the remains of my grandparents' old house," said Noé. "I thought it used to be around here."

"Well, there was once another house here," said Castro. "But there was a terrible tragedy. Do you know about this?"

"I know that the house was supposed to have burned, that my grandparents lost almost everything."

"That's right," affirmed the man, drinking his own glass of water. "It was left in a state of disorder for a long time. Until . . . what did you say your name was?"

"I'm sorry. I am Noé Carabajál Quintanilla. My mother is Estela Quintanilla Carabajál."

"I think I know your brother, Gabriel," said Castro. "In fact, that is why I am here."

"My brother? I never knew him, I'm afraid. My mother took me with her to Mexico City when I was very small."

"Yes. I think I knew that. So you grew up there! What an exciting life. Isn't it?" Castro asked nervously. "Would you like some more water? We have our own well."

"No, thank you. But I am interested in what you have here. Is this a church?"

"Yes, Evangelical. Your brother came back, I started to say, some years after your mother—you and your mother—left. He cleared the rubble from the fire and helped build this church. He used to stand on the stones, the foundation of the house, and preach."

"Preach?"

"Yes, he is a minister. He has since started many churches. He is responsible for the salvation of many souls."

"So he is no longer here, in Saltillo."

"No, he asked me to take over this church. He had left his family in Texas or Arizona, and returned to them. Since your mother left, I don't think that there was much here for him."

"She never talks about him," said Noé. "So I didn't really know what had happened. There is a lot she hasn't told me."

"Well, that's how families are sometimes," said Castro, relieved now that the subject had been broached. "But the Reverend Carabajál has kept you, all of you, in his prayers."

"Well, I am thankful for that."

Noé stood as though to leave.

"Wait!" said Castro. "I have one thing to show you, that might interest you." He disappeared into the back room of the house, where Noé assumed that the family slept. There was an open kitchen tacked onto the side of the house, and a cool breeze wafted through, blowing the little white curtains on the windows. He noted a small podium in a corner, and a table with a red and gold cloth upon it that said, HE IS RISEN! He assumed that these were pulled out from the wall when the room served as a gathering place for the little congregation. There was no crucifix anywhere in the room, and Noé thought that this was a curious church, indeed.

Castro returned with a little book. He tried to rub something off of the cover, and when Noé took it in his hands, he saw that it was soot.

"I thought you might want to have this. Gabriel found it when we were clearing the remains of the other house."

Noé opened the book, then paged carefully through to the back, where he found a title page. The book was in Hebrew.

"I wish that I could read it," said Noé. "I recognize some of the characters from my grandfather's descriptions, but he is blind now, and cannot teach me."

"It is part of your legacy," said Castro. "You should take it."

"Why didn't my brother keep it?"

Castro pondered the question. "I think he felt that it belonged here, that this was a fitting place for it. He reads a little Hebrew, you know. And Greek. He has taught himself."

"Perhaps I should, too," said Noé. He weighed the little book in his hand, wondering if he should take it to his grandfather. He was frail now, not long for this world.

Finally, he handed it back to the Reverend Castro. "I think my brother is right," he said. "It belongs here."

"Bueno," said Castro. "Then here it will remain. But if you change your mind, you know where it is."

"Thank you," said Noé. "And good luck with your work."

"Thank you," said Castro. "God bless you."

Noé walked away from the little house, stopping once to view it from the road. From here he could see an old fountain to one side, moving in and out of deep shadow as the overgrown trees around it swayed gently in the wind.

THE COVENANT

hen Noé returned to the Capital, he sent word to La Señorita that his mother, La Viuda Carabajál, would not be returning from Saltillo. He did not receive a response immediately, which did not concern him, as La Señorita was often preoccupied with many matters at once.

Noé wrote two stories for the dailies, as he needed the money, then gathered up the copy for the current issue of *La Linterna* to deliver to the printer. He called first at the home of his grandparents, to see if they were well, and to inquire as to the current location of M Cardoz' premises.

"He is gone," said Mariana.

"Who is gone?" asked Noé, fearing the worst.

"The printer, the man who prints the papers for your mother. No one has seen him."

Noé breathed a sigh of relief. "The printer? I'm sure he is fine. Probably just being cautious. He is not gone. He is not an old man, unless he had an accident."

Mariana shook her head. "No one knows when death will come for us."

Noé kissed her papery cheek. "It will never come for you, Nona. You will be translated directly to heaven like the saints."

She shook her head again. "No heaven for me. This has been my heaven, life with your grandfather on this earth."

"Where is he?" asked Noé.

"In the garden."

Noé found his grandfather seated on a low bench in the sun. A scruffy cat was allowing the old man to rub its back. "Where have you been?" asked Julio. "We have missed you."

"And I have missed you, too," said Noé. "I accompanied my mother back to Saltillo. She has decided to stay there, with her sister, my aunt Blanca."

"Ah, Saltillo," said Julio, like an exhalation of air from the past. He sat quietly for a few minutes, as though reliving his life there. "I miss my garden."

"But this is a wonderful garden," said Noé. "And I would not have known you all my life if you had not come here."

"Yes," said Julio, turning his blind eyes towards Noé. "Or perhaps you would not have come here yourself, with your mother."

Noé could neither refute nor confirm this, so he said nothing at all. The past was too complex for him to disentangle, like roots growing thickly in a pot. They listened for a moment to the gurglings of the squat fountain at the center of the courtyard.

"I need to find the printer," said Noé finally, "and finish one last project for my mother."

Julio did not volunteer to seek out this information. "Do not look too hard," was his response. "Or you may find him after all."

It was not like Noé's grandparents to dissemble, so he decided to call upon La Señorita and see if she had any information on the printer's whereabouts. Noé hurried to the house on Paseo de Bucareli. There he found Humberto, looking tired, sitting in his familiar place in La Señorita's study.

"She is gone," said Humberto. "She died while visiting a friend in the countryside."

Humberto looked towards her customary seat on the velvet divan, and the room suddenly seemed empty without her vital presence. A vase of blood red roses stood on a low side table.

"I can't believe it," said Noé. "I especially cannot believe this happened while we were gone."

"Neither can I," said Humberto. "I think we all expected her to live forever. Men old enough to be my father said that they had known her when they were children, and she looked exactly the same." He paused and looked out the window at the gracious courtyard, the bubbling fountain. Noé looked, too. He had played there all of his life, could even now hear La Señorita's imperious voice giving orders to three different people at once.

Then Humberto returned his gaze to Noé. "Come back on the twelfth. That is the day of the reading of the will. I am the executor, and it is important that you be here."

"My mother is not returning," he said. "I think that she will stay in Saltillo."

"Your mother's presence is not required," said Humberto. "I think that La Señorita foresaw that possibility when you left. I suggest that you go to your apartment and return on the twelfth, when the reading of the will takes place."

Noé started to speak.

"But there are conditions," said Humberto, stopping Noé's further questions, "that will be revealed when the will is read."

✳

Noé returned to his apartment, where he found Samuel. "Where have you been?" asked Samuel. "Many things have happened while you have been gone."

"So I gather," said Noé.

"Don Porfírio and his Special Police have decided that enough free journalism is enough," said Samuel. "Several people have been arrested. I would avoid the printer, if I were you."

Noé was frustrated. He had promised his mother he would deliver this one last set of proofs to the mysterious M Cardoz. Also, by this time, his curiosity was piqued. "Do you think the printer's disappearance has anything to do with the police?"

"I can't say," answered Samuel. "But anything is possible."

Noé decided to take a stroll through La Colonia Condesa, towards El Hipodromo, in the hopes of seeing or hearing something that might be useful to him. He noted when the portly man in the bowler hat began to walk about a block behind him, but this did not worry him. He recognized the man from previous strolls, and knew that he was easy to lose, as the man was loathe to get his shoes dirty or to climb over obstacles higher than his waist.

Noé stopped and visited with people along the way, street vendors and other habitual strollers, people who might have seen the printer's sign posted in a door or alleyway, or might know the printer by other affiliations. These latter were more furtive, and did not encourage him to linger and make conversation with them.

When Noé was satisfied that the printer could not be located, he left his pursuer in a convenient dead end, blocked from view by the passage of an ostentatious carriage. But Noé had failed to note the second follower, who clubbed Noé as he stood lighting his pipe, then caught his falling body and placed it in that same carriage. As Noé fell, he caught a glimpse of the man in the bowler hat, and kicked out with all his strength at the smug and leering face.

✳

And now I sit in my prison cell, not this time in the "writers' salon"—the better quarters in which I had been held before. This time I am closer to the bottom of the building, where the rats are more numerous, and foul water drips from above. I do not know what day it is. In fact, I do not know if it is day or night. No one has called on me, and I doubt that anyone knows I am here.

Far off, somewhere above me, I hear the shrieks of a woman, either shrieks of terror, or the result of drunkenness. The men and women are held in adjacent quarters, with a mere blanket between them, so any abomination is possible. Had I, at least, the little money I was carrying when I was picked up, I could have paid for better quarters and food, but when I regained consciousness, my pockets were empty.

The Chief of the Special Police, during several long and fascinating conversations, requested that I write a confession, and so left me the paper and pen that I was carrying at the time of my abduction. Curiously, when I refused to comply, he proceeded to lovingly and thoroughly break the bones of my right hand. This may be order, but it is definitely not progress. My only satisfaction is that I seem to have broken the nose of Special Policeman Arnoldo Gutiérrez, the man in the bowler hat, who was present at the first of our sessions, no doubt to attest to my innate viciousness and antisocial attitude.

The last issue of La Linterna, which I was carrying with me upon my last day of freedom, was also taken as evidence of my corruption and crimes against the state, as the Chief put it. Thank God that all of the names therein are false, and that no one can be implicated by the contents.

In spite of these setbacks, and having nothing better to do with my time here, I have done as my mother instructed, no, begged of me in our days together: to write down everything that transpired in her life just as she told it to me. I have begun this by use of my left hand, which has not been an easy task.

In addition, however, I have written down the events that I myself have witnessed, from the lavender smell of the jacaranda trees in my grandparents' garden, to the stench of corruption and decay that fills my nostrils even now. I use the smooth pages of stationery that had once proclaimed the printery of M Cardoz across the top. The ink has now all but faded, but if I hold a sheet up to the light, I can just make out a faint script, like the scratchings of lost Sanskrit, across the page.

Having done all this, I await the Deluge.

✱

Noé was released from Belem before the Deluge, but after several months had passed. No explanation was given, neither for his detention nor his release. He made his way back to his apartment, where he found a family occupying the flat. He knocked at the door of the casera.

She did not smile or greet him when she opened the door. "We had to ask your friend to leave," she said. "The police kept coming around and asking questions. We can't afford that kind of attention."

"Do you know where he went?" asked Noé. "Do you know where my belongings are?"

The casera was looking at his bandaged hands. "No," she said, "they took everything," and closed the door.

Noé then went to the house of Dr. Gonsález, hoping to find Samuel, or at least an address for him. The professor himself answered the door.

"Profesor!" said Noé, happy to see a familiar face.

Gonsález smiled. "Noé!" he said. "I am glad to see you alive. I had heard that you might be released soon."

"Who helped secure my freedom?" he asked.

"Well, your editors did not abandon you completely," said Gonsález, "and they had other help as well."

"You mean monetary?"

"I suppose so," said Gonsález.

"Well, please thank those people, if you can, for me."

There was an awkward silence as Noé realized that Gonsález was not going to invite him in. "Please, can you tell me where I can find Samuel?"

"We have sent him to stay with relatives in Aguascalientes for a while," he said, "until things cool off. It has been a bad time for everyone."

Noé felt a sudden chill. "Then I will not bother you any longer. And my things?"

"Ah, they are at the home of La Señorita. What's left of them, anyway," said Gonsález. "I'm afraid that the Special Police went through them rather thoroughly." He reached into his pocket and pulled out some money. "Here. Hire a carriage. It is too far to walk."

Noé did not refuse him.

Noé climbed down from the carriage and made his way to the expansive doorway of La Señorita's home. It had been several months since his last visit. He had not returned for the reading of the will.

After ringing the bell at the door, he waited a bit. Suddenly he felt very tired and realized that he had not eaten all day. He could hear workers inside and wondered what changes were being made. He thought of the parlor with its gatherings full of sparkling laughter, then of the little room with the foxhunt painted around the walls.

The door was opened by someone he did not recognize. She had her hair pulled back in a practical braid but was not wearing the apron of a maid.

"Good afternoon," he began, "my name is Noé Carabajál." Then he realized who she was. "Princesa," he said. Meaning to bow in exaggerated courtesy, he instead sank weakly to his knees.

"There is no need to prostrate yourself," she said, reaching out to lift him up. "My name is Matilda. No royal title, just Matilda."

He looked into her eyes. "Matilda," he said faintly. "Why are you here?"

"I work here," she said. "La Señorita hired me to replace your mother just before she died."

"You are . . . La Directora? And what is your last name, Matilda?"

"I have none," she said. "I have no family. I had to come here in order to gain any name at all."

She led Noé into the alcove where La Señorita used to do her business and Humberto had kept his office. It was now stripped of most of its furnishings. Workmen were in an adjacent room, restoring the walls.

"What happened?" he asked.

"Remember that monstrosity of an organ that used to be in the parlor? Humberto said that the women in the orchestra refused to have anything to do with it. It is just as well. It caught fire one night and almost burned down the house."

"Any particular night?" asked Noé.

"Yes. The night La Señorita died."

This did not surprise him.

"Shall I bring you something to drink? You look pale."

"If that would not be too much trouble." The young woman left him sitting in the front room. He was finding it hard to believe that there were not servants to do these things. He wondered what had become of Humberto.

Matilda returned with a tray. On it were some slices of papaya with lime and a tall glass of juice. "I'm afraid this is all there is," she said. "And there is no silverware. The creditors took it."

Behind her came Humberto, as if summoned by Noé's thoughts, covered in plaster dust. "Noé," said Humberto. He reached to shake his hand, then hugged him instead. "I am so glad you have come. Please have some refreshments."

Noé ate and drank as Humberto and Matilda discussed the remodeling of the house. "I hope you don't mind," said Humberto, "that we took the liberty of beginning repairs. We wanted to forestall further damage from the weather."